Lynne Graham was born in Northern Ireland and has been a keen romance reader since her teens. She is very happily married, to an understanding husband who has learned to cook since she started to write! Her five children keep her on her toes. She has a very large dog, who knocks everything over, a very small terrier, who barks a lot, and two cats. When time allows, Lynne is a keen gardener.

THE GREEK'S
SURPRISE
CHRISTMAS
BRIDE

LYNNE GRAHAM

MILLS & BOON

First Published in Great Britain 2019
by Mills & Boon, an imprint of HarperCollins*Publishers*
1 London Bridge Street, London, SE1 9GF

© 2019 Lynne Graham

ISBN: 978-0-263-27111-9

MIX
Paper from
responsible sources
FSC® C007454

This book is produced from independently certified FSC™ paper
to ensure responsible forest management.
For more information visit www.harpercollins.co.uk/green.

Printed and bound in Spain
by CPI, Barcelona

CHAPTER ONE

LEO ROMANOS, BILLIONAIRE shipping heir, woke up at dawn with four children in his enormous bed.

He had freaked out the first time it had happened, bought pyjamas for the first time ever and hired a twenty-four-hour, round-the-clock rota of nannies.

But the nanny rota wasn't working. His late sister's traumatised kids still got out of bed in the middle of the night and slunk into his, and they brought the babies as well.

It was a wonder that *he* wasn't traumatised, Leo reflected in wonderment. Five-year-old Popi had ten-month-old Theon tucked in her arms, and three-year-old Sybella had two-year-old Cosmo clasped next to her. His nephews and nieces weren't happy, weren't secure—in spite of all his efforts to make a home for them.

And for their benefit alone Leo was willing, finally, to make the ultimate sacrifice. He would take a wife prepared to be a mother to his four inherited children.

His father and stepmother had refused to take charge of their grandkids and had signed over their guardianship to Leo, his stepmother insisting that his father was too old for the task. And, in truth, Leo hadn't appreciated the extent of the challenge he was taking on.

He had assumed that the nannies would enable him to return to his normal life: workaholic hours followed by the occasional party or dinner, and regular visits to his very sexy mistress. Only somehow it wasn't working out that way. Leo's wonderfully smooth and self-indulgent life had gone to hell when his five-year-old niece had sobbed as if her heart was breaking because he'd said he wouldn't be home for dinner.

Guilt and more guilt had dogged him in spades ever since.

The children needed more than he was capable of giving them—which meant he had to step up, take a wife, and give the kids a mother who would do all the things he didn't want to do and keep them happy while allowing him an uninterrupted night of sleep.

He suppressed a groan, knowing exactly where he would head to find that wife. Six years ago he had been offered a bride from the Livas family—a practical dynastic marriage which would have ended the competition between the two shipping companies, amalgamated them and made him the heir to both empires. The alliance had offered him an enormous profit and tremendous prospects and the proposed bride had been a beauty...

But even so he had hesitated. Leo had loved his freedom and still did, and the potential bride had hinted at a dangerous desire for his fidelity and he had baulked at that tripwire and backed off fast.

Leo had been raised in the belief that marriage was for business, property and heirs, all that sort of legal stuff. There was no room in marriage for the adventurous sex and variety which Leo considered to be an absolute essential of life, so he had stepped back. But four troubled, needy children crawling into his bed made him far less exacting in his expectations. As far as he knew, Elexis Livas was still on the market and suddenly he was willing to consider a deal…

Isidore Livas met him in his Athens office, a very traditional setting, far removed from Leo's very contemporary place of business in the City of London. He was quick to inform Leo that his daughter, Elexis, was on the brink of an engagement and no longer available. Leo suppressed a sigh, not of disappointment because his current mistress was considerably sexier than Elexis; however, he had warmed to the concept of marrying her because she was vaguely familiar to him.

'However, I have a granddaughter,' Isidore admitted grudgingly, surprising Leo with that information. 'As I'm sure you're aware, my son went off the rails…'

Leo nodded, for the world and his wife were aware that Julian Livas, product of his father's first marriage, had taken to drugs and drink and manic bad behaviour from an early age. He had died in his twenties from his excesses. Isidore had Elexis later in life, with his second wife.

'Two months ago, I learned to my surprise that Julian *did* have a child with a woman in London. He didn't marry the woman concerned, so my grandchild was born out of wedlock,' Isidore revealed with old-fashioned distaste. 'Letty is twenty-four and single. You can still become my heir if you take her as a bride… I have no one else, Leo. Elexis's chosen husband is a television presenter with no interest in taking over my business, and I would very much like to retire.'

'And this… Letty?' Leo questioned with a frown, for he considered it an ugly name.

The older man grimaced. 'You couldn't compare her to Elexis. She's plain and plump but she'd marry you like a shot because she needs money for her family.'

'Plain and plump' didn't exactly thrill Leo either. He mightn't want a wife for entertainment in the bedroom but, understandably, he wanted a presentable woman. His black brows drew together in complete puzzlement. 'Why aren't *you* helping her family?'

The expression on Isidore's thin face shuttered. 'She approached me for help but, as far as I'm concerned, if my son wasn't prepared to marry her mother, I shouldn't be expected to provide for their child, now that the girl's an adult.'

'And yet you're willing to make this girl your heiress,' Leo remarked wryly.

'*If* she marries you. That's different. She has Livas blood in her veins and I will accept her then. But she's lowborn,' Isidore murmured broodingly. 'She doesn't speak Greek. She has not been raised with our traditions and you may not find that palatable. She works as a care assistant in a home for the elderly.'

Leo's brain could not even encompass the concept of a wife who worked in so humble a capacity. Born with the proverbial silver spoon in his mouth to a family who had enjoyed wealth for generations, he had no experience whatsoever of what it was like to be born poor. 'In your opinion is your granddaughter likely to be the maternal type?'

'If you can judge her by the way she fights and

argues in favour of her siblings' welfare, I would say so...'

Leo was frowning again. 'Siblings? Julian had *more* than one child with her mother?'

'No. Only Letty is Julian's child. Her mother had the two younger boys with another man,' Isidore clarified with compressed lips. 'I gather that relationship didn't last either and now the mother is ill or disabled or something.'

'Tell Letty what I have to offer and send her to me,' Leo advised with all the arrogance of his wealthy forebears. 'I am willing to marry her if I find her acceptable but, for the children's sake, she *must* be a good woman.'

An unexpected laugh erupted from Isidore, startling the older man almost as much as it startled Leo, who had always viewed Isidore as humourless. 'Leo...what would *you* know about *good* women?'

Faint colour accentuated the high exotic slant of Leo's cheekbones and he lifted a brow and nodded in grudging acknowledgement of that accurate question. Even so, he was very conscious of his duty towards his nephews and nieces and he was determined not to land them with a nasty stepmother, such as he had had to endure. In truth, however, he knew much more about calculating, cruel and greedy women than he knew about the other type.

On his flight back to London, Leo decided to look into Letty and have her investigated but was instead forced to have her late father's history explored because Isidore had neglected to give him Letty's surname. By the time he arrived back in London, a file awaited him and the information within was unexpectedly interesting. Juliet, known as Letty, Harbison was a much more thought-provoking bride-to-be than her socialite Aunt Elexis had ever been. Leo's rarely roused curiosity was stimulated.

Unaware of the high-flying plans afoot for her future, Letty stared at the loan shark on their doorstep. 'You're breaking the law,' she told him sharply. 'You are not allowed to harass and intimidate your debtors.'

'I'm entitled to ask for my money,' he told her fiercely, a thin little man in a crumpled suit, another man, unshaven and thuggish in shape, poised behind him, his sidekick, Joe, who had attempted to thump her little brother for trying to stand up to him on his last visit. He had backed off when Letty wielded the cricket bat she kept behind the door.

'You'll have your payment as soon as I get paid, just like last month and the month before,' Letty responded, squaring her shoulders, honey-blonde hair caught up in a ponytail bouncing with the movement, her green eyes clear and steady. 'I can't give you what I don't have.'

'A little bird told me you have rich relations.'

An angry flush illuminated Letty's creamy skin as she wondered if one of her brothers had let that dangerous cat out of the bag. 'I asked. He wouldn't help.'

'He might help soon enough if you was unlucky enough to have an…accident,' Joe piped up ungrammatically, baring crooked teeth in a smile that was a grimace of threat.

'But if I were to have an accident, you wouldn't be getting any money at all,' Letty pointed out flatly and closed the door swiftly, seeing no advantage to continuing the dialogue.

'Rich relations', she thought wryly, thinking back to her one meeting with her Greek grandfather, when he had visited London on business. A cold, unfriendly man more hung up on the reality that she was illegitimate rather than showing any genuine interest in her actual existence. No, contacting Isidore Livas had been a dead end. She had soon worked out that no rescue bid would be coming from him. He had shaken her off like the poor relation she was.

While her mother, Gillian, hobbled painfully round the tiny kitchen of their council flat on crutches and tried to tidy up, Letty made a cheap but nutritious evening meal for her family. Her two brothers sat at the table in the living room, both of them engaged in homework. Tim was thirteen and Kyle was nine. Letty considered her half-brothers marginally less useless than she considered the rest of the world's men.

There were no towering heroes in Letty's depressing experience of men. Her father, Julian, had been a handsome, irresponsible lightweight, incapable of fighting his addictions to toxic substances. He had lived with her mother and her only once and for a brief period, after a more than usually successful stay in a rehab facility, but within months he had fallen off the wagon again and that had been the last Letty had seen of him.

Yet, tragically, meeting Julian Livas had derailed her mother's entire life. Gillian had been a middle-class schoolgirl at the exclusive co-educational boarding school where she had met Julian. A teenage pregnancy had resulted and when Gillian had refused to have a termination her parents had thrown her out and washed their hands of her. Letty had always respected the hard struggle Gillian had faced, simply to survive as a young mother. As a single parent, Gillian had sub-sequently trained as a nurse and life had been stable until Gillian fell in love again.

Letty grimaced as she thought of her stepfather, Robbie, a steady worker and a likeable man but, un-derneath the surface show of decency and reliability, a hopeless womaniser. When Gillian could no longer live with his lies and deceptions, they had had to move on and inevitably their standard of living had gone down-hill with the divorce. In his own way, Robbie had been as feckless as her father, although he did maintain a stable relationship with his two sons.

Letty had worked very hard at school, determined that she would never have to rely on a man for support. And what good had it done her? she asked herself rue-fully. It had given her a scholarship to a top sixth form college and the chance to study medicine at Oxford but, within a few years, just as Letty was starting to stretch her wings into independence and the promise of a satisfying career, misfortune had rolled back in and her family had needed her back at home to bring in a living wage.

She had been three years into her medical degree when Gillian's worsening arthritis had forced her to give up work and live on benefits. Undaunted, Gillian had retrained as a drug and alcohol counsellor, who could work from a wheelchair, but all it took was a broken lift in their tower apartment block—and it was frequently out of order—and she was trapped indoors and unable either to work or to earn. That one very bleak Christmas, when Letty was in the fifth year of her course, Gillian had got involved in the murky un-

derworld of unsecured loans and had fallen into debt
as the interest charges mushroomed.

Letty rode into work on the elderly motorbike she
had restored. Parking her bike and securing it, she
walked into the Sunset Home for the Elderly, where
she worked as the permanent night shift manager. She
was on a good salary and had no complaints about her
working conditions or colleagues. She had every intention of completing her medical studies as soon as
it was possible but, right at that moment, that desired
goal seemed worryingly distant. Her mother was too
frail to be left alone with two active boys until she received the double hip replacement she needed. Sadly,
the waiting lists for free treatment were too long and
private surgery was unaffordable. In the short term,
more accessible accommodation would have much improved Gillian's lot and her ability to work but the large
debt that she had accrued with that iniquitous loan had
to be cleared before moving could even be considered.

As Letty changed out of bike leathers into work
garb, her phone started ringing and she answered it
swiftly, always fearful of her mother having suffered
a fall, which would exacerbate her condition. But it
wasn't one of her brothers calling to give her bad news,
it was, amazingly, her grandfather.

'If you're willing to do whatever it takes to help your
family, Leo is the man to approach. I will text you the
phone number. Furthermore, if you were to reach an
agreement with Leo, I will invite you into my home
and introduce you to Greek society,' the older man informed her loftily in the tone of someone who believed
he was offering her some great honour.

'Er…right. Thanks for that,' Letty responded ruefully, wondering why her grandfather would think that she was interested in being introduced to Greek society and what sort of agreement he believed she could reach with this guy, Leo, that was likely to benefit her or her family. Maybe the older man wasn't as cold a fish as she had assumed, and he was genuinely trying to help her. She was too much of a cynic for a wannabe doctor, she scolded herself, she really had to start trying harder to see the good in human beings.

The next morning, before she headed home to bed after her shift, she took out the number and phoned it.

'VR Shipping,' a woman answered.

'My name is Letty Harbison. I have to make an appointment with someone called Leo?'

'If you will excuse me for a moment…' the woman urged.

Letty groaned at the sound of voices fussing in the background. Was this Leo likely to offer her better paid employment? He was obviously a businessman in an office environment. When she got home, she would look him up online, although she would need more than his first name to accomplish that, she reflected wearily.

'Mr Romanos will see you at ten this morning at his London office.' The woman then read out the address of his building.

'I'm sorry, I'm a night shift worker and it would need to be a little later in the day,' Letty began apologetically.

'Mr Romanos will not be available later. He is a very busy man.'

Letty rolled her eyes. 'Ten will be fine,' she conceded, reasoning that it was only sensible to check the man out because her grandfather *could* genuinely be attempting to do her a good turn. *And pigs might fly*, her inner cynic sniped as she remembered the single cup of black coffee she had enjoyed in the fancy restaurant where she had met her father's father for the first time for a twenty-minute chat which had consisted of his barked questions and her laboured replies.

It had been a painful meeting because she had truly hoped that there would be some sense of family connection between them, but there had been nothing, only an older man, evidently still very bitter about his only son's early death. Even worse, any reference Letty had made to her family's problems had only seemed to increase her grandfather's contempt for her and her mother and brothers.

Dragging herself out of the recollection of that disheartening conversation, she checked the time and suppressed another groan. There was no way on earth she could get home, freshen up and change and then catch the bus to make that appointment in time. Oh, to heck with that, she thought in sudden rebellion, she would attend the appointment as she was, in her bike leathers, and explain that she had just left work and had nothing else to wear. After calling her mother to warn her that she would be late back, Letty climbed back on her bike.

'Have you a parcel?' the receptionist asked Letty on her arrival in the building.

'No, I have an appointment with Mr Leo… Romanos, is it? At ten,' she recited uncertainly because she had been so drowsy when she had made that initial call that her concentration and powers of recall were not operating with their usual efficiency.

The top floor receptionist's eyes rounded as she took in Letty in her biker leathers because she was a gossip and, according to the grapevine, Leo Romanos had unexpectedly cancelled a very important meeting to clear a last-minute space for a female visitor. The usual lively speculation about his sex life had duly erupted in a frenzy. Only, sadly, Letty did not fit the bill because Leo was a living legend for his taste in beautiful women, who were invariably models or socialites, spiced with the occasional actress. Nobody looking at Letty could possibly have placed her in any of those categories.

Letty sank down on a squashy and very comfortable sofa in the reception area and the exhaustion she suffered by never ever getting enough rest simply engulfed her in a drowning tide. Her sleepy eyes executed one last final sweep of the ultra-modern, very luxurious floor of offices and wonderment assailed her. Why on earth had her grandfather sent her to such a place? Yes, she had the usual office skills but she seriously doubted they would be on a par with the kind of commercial skills employees needed to have in a business environment. Even worse, she was dressed all wrong, had only just managed to get out of the lift before being asked if she had brought the pizzas someone was awaiting. She had been mistaken for a takeaway delivery person.

'Your ten o'clock appointment is asleep in Reception,' one of Leo's assistants informed him.

Asleep? *Theos*…how was she contriving to sleep on the brink of potentially meeting her future husband? It did not occur to Leo that Isidore Livas would have been foolish enough to send his granddaughter to see him without that all-important proposal having being outlined in advance. He hadn't expected to meet her quite so quickly, however, had assumed it would take at least a week to set up such a meeting. He was allowing the necessary time for Letty to make whatever effort she could to look her best to meet the expectations of a billionaire seeking a bride.

Leo strode out to Reception, disconcerting everyone, turning every head, and then he saw her, lying full length along the sofa, very nearly merging with the black upholstery in her leathers. Leather? Why was she dressed from top to toe in leather and wearing chunky motorbike boots?

Bemused, Leo came to a halt and stared down at her, noticing the long messy ponytail, so long it almost brushed the floor. She had long honey-blonde hair. All the Livas tribe were some shade of blonde, he recalled abstractedly as his roaming attention mounted the curve of a lush pouting derrière sleekly outlined by leather and a long slender thigh. Her face was pillowed on her hand, sleep-flushed, her lips full and pink. She wasn't very tall. In fact she was short in stature, another Livas trait. She might be lucky to reach his chest, even in high heels. But she wasn't plain and she certainly wasn't plump. She was simply wonderfully curved in all the right feminine places and only a man with a wife and a daughter the size and shape of toothpicks could have deemed Letty plump, Leo reflected wryly. Involuntarily, he was still staring because he wanted to know what lay below the leather jacket she had zipped up tight and he was ridiculously tempted to scoop her up and just carry her into his office. Courtesy, however, would be the wiser choice and Leo was usually wise.

'Letty...' Leo intoned in his deep dark drawl. *'Letty...'*

Theos, he hated that name, which was more suited to an Edwardian kitchen maid and Juliet was so much prettier. *He* would call her Juliet.

Letty shifted position and her lashes fluttered as she forced her unwilling body back to wakefulness when all it wanted to do was sleep. She began to push herself up on her arm and her eyes widened on the man poised at the end of the sofa. He was so disconcerting a vision that she blinked, expecting him to vanish like the illusion he had to be. But he stayed steady, a very tall, lean and powerful figure, garbed in a business suit so exquisitely tailored to his exact physique that he looked like a model, a male supermodel who would have looked more at home with the backdrop of a vast yacht behind him.

He had black cropped hair, razor-edged cheekbones and a perfect nose and mouth. As for the eyes, well, Letty, who never went into raptures, could've gone into raptures over those dark deep-set eyes glimmering with rich honey accents and framed by ridiculously long lashes. Letty wasn't even surprised that she was staring, she, who never stared at a man, unless it was in an attempt to intimidate him. He was an outrageously beautiful male specimen and quite dazzlingly noticeable.

He stretched down a hand. 'I'm Leo Romanos,' he informed her with quiet hauteur.

She couldn't wait to look him up online and find out all about him, although it was clear that he shared her grandfather's arrogance even if he wore it differently. Leo Romanos, she sensed, was a man accustomed to having others leap to do his bidding and he took it quite for granted. Isidore Livas, however, didn't project quite the same level of expectation and intimidation, and felt the need to frown and pitch his voice louder to make a similar impression.

'Letty Harbison...' Letty said, belatedly recalling her manners, heated embarrassment momentarily claiming her as she realised she had been sleeping full length along the sofa in a public place. Then, in common with most junior doctors, Letty could've fallen asleep standing up on one leg, particularly after several sessions spent observing, fetching and carrying in a busy emergency unit.

'Is there somewhere I could...freshen up?' she asked, evading that shrewd dark gaze of his, her defences kicking in because she had stared at him—she didn't *stare* at men and didn't feel comfortable with the fact that she had stared at him.

He indicated the cloakroom behind the waiting area and she shot upright, learning that he was even taller than she had suspected and surprised even more to learn that there *were* men around who could make her feel positively small and dainty.

She vanished into the cloakroom at speed, grimacing when she caught her pink and tousled reflection. In an effort to tidy her hair she tugged off her hairband and it snapped, leaving her with a wealth of honey-blonde tresses spilling untidily over her shoulders. She cursed and threw her head back to shift her mane of hair down her back before unzipping and removing her jacket because she was much too hot. She washed her hands, briefly wished she had brought a lipstick with her and suppressed the idle thought again. It would take more than a dash of lipstick to make her look like an efficient and elegant office worker in VR Shipping, where even the receptionist resembled a Miss World contender.

'This way, please…' another employee greeted her when she emerged. 'I'll show you to Mr Romanos's office. Would you like some coffee?'

'Yes, thank you,' Letty responded warmly, thinking that coffee, which she rarely drank, might wake her up because, after that short burst of sleep, her brain cells felt as though they were drowning in sludge. 'I take it black, no sugar.'

Leo had a vague unrealistic hope that Juliet would reappear looking rather more conventional and even wearing a little make-up and carting a bag of some kind like a normal woman. Instead, she came through the door, carrying her jacket with her hair loose. And what hair it was, Leo marvelled, watching the luxuriant honey-blonde strands flick against her shapely hips as she turned to shut the door behind her. She spun back, eyes as green as fresh ferns in sunlight, alert and questioning now, and she gripped her jacket even closer to her chest, as though she was trying to conceal the undeniably magnificent swell of her breasts below the plain black T-shirt she wore.

Leo liked curvy women, but he loved the female breast in all sizes and, as she settled down in the chair set in front of his desk, he was enchanted by the very slight bounce of her bosom as she sat down. Natural curves, he was convinced, not bought and paid for, shaped by some talented surgeon. Encountering her gaze, Leo went as hard as a rock and it shocked him, sincerely shocked him, because *that* didn't happen to him any more in public. He strode around his desk to take a seat, disconcerted by that juvenile response to a woman who was fully clothed, bare of make-up and, so far, not even a little flirtatious or suggestive.

His assistant entered with a tray of coffee and poured it.

'I don't usually drink coffee, but I need it to wake me up this morning,' Letty admitted with a rueful smile that lit up her oval face. 'I apologise for not being more smartly dressed but I only finished work at eight and there wasn't time to go home and change and get back here in time.'

'Why the biker leathers?'

'I use a motorbike to get around. It's cheap to run and perfect for getting through rush hour traffic,' Letty explained, sipping the coffee she held between her cupped hands. 'I don't know why my grandfather insisted that I should come and see you. Do you have some sort of work that I could do? A job to offer?'

Leo froze, belatedly registering that Isidore had not done the footwork for him. 'I have a proposition that you may wish to consider.'

'Did Isidore mention that I'm in need of money?' Letty had to force herself to ask, her creamy skin turning pink with self-consciousness.

'Your grandfather asked you to call him Isidore?' Leo remarked in surprise.

'Oh, he didn't invite me to call him anything,' Letty parried with rueful amusement. 'To be frank, he didn't want to acknowledge the relationship.'

'That must've been a disappointment,' Leo commented wryly.

'Not really. I wasn't expecting a miracle but, considering that my father never paid any child support, it's not as though I've cost that side of my family anything over the years,' she responded quietly. 'My mother has always been very independent but right now that's not possible for her, so I've had to step in…'

'Which is where I enter the equation from your point of view,' Leo incised. 'Your grandfather wants to amalgamate his shipping firm with mine and retire, leaving me in charge. For me, the price of that valuable alliance is that I marry you.'

A pin-drop silence fell.

'You would have to marry *me* to get his shipping business?' Letty exclaimed in disbelief. 'I've never heard anything so outrageous in my life! I knew he was an out-of-date old codger, but I didn't realise he was *insane*!'

'Then I must be insane too,' Leo acknowledged smoothly. 'Because I am willing to agree to that deal, although I also have more pressing reasons for being currently in need of a wife…'

Letty felt disorientated and bewildered. 'You *need* a wife?' she almost whispered, wondering why there wasn't a stampede of eager women pushing her out of their path to reach him and then suppressing that weird and frivolous thought, irritated by her lapse in concentration.

'Six months ago, my sister and her husband died in a car crash. I am attempting to raise their four children. I need a wife to help me with that task,' Leo spelt out succinctly.

'*Four*…children?' Letty gasped in consternation.

'Aged five and under.' Leo decided to give her all the bad news at once. 'The baby was a newborn, who was premature at birth. Ben and Anastasia were on the way to pick him up and finally bring him home from the hospital when they were killed.'

In the stretching heavy silence, Letty blinked in shock. 'How tragic...'

'Yes, but rather more tragic for their children, with only me to fall back on. They need a mother figure, someone who's there more often. I work long hours and I travel as well. The set-up that I have at the moment is not working well enough for them.'

Letty shrugged a slight fatalistic shoulder. 'So, you make sacrifices. You change your lifestyle.'

'I have already done that. Bringing in a wife to share the responsibility makes better sense,' Leo declared in a tone of finality as though only he could give an opinion in that field.

'And you and my grandfather, who doesn't really *want* to be my grandfather,' Letty suggested with a rueful curve to her soft mouth, 'somehow reached the conclusion that *I* could be that wife?'

'You are Isidore's only option, his sole available female relative. His daughter's about to get engaged.'

'So, my Aunt Elexis wasn't ready to snap you up,' Letty observed.

Leo compressed his wide sensual mouth at her slightly mocking intonation. 'Isidore first approached me on her behalf six years ago. I said no.'

'You said no,' Letty echoed weakly, struggling without success to get into the thought patterns of rich Greeks, prepared to marry purely to unite their companies and families.

'I'm only willing to marry now to benefit the children,' Leo told her.

'But marriage is a lot more intimate in nature than an agreement to raise children together,' Letty pointed out.

Leo lounged fluidly back in his chair. 'In our case, it would be *less* intimate. Sex wouldn't be involved. I would satisfy my needs elsewhere.'

Letty turned bright red and she didn't know why. After all, she knew everything there was to know about the mechanics of sex, hormones and physical needs, even if she did lack actual experience. 'So, you wouldn't require sex from your wife?' she checked, not quite sure she could credit that.

'No. I keep a mistress for that purpose. It's more convenient,' Leo informed her without shame or an ounce of embarrassment.

Letty shook her head as if to clear it. Possibly it was to convince herself that this unusual conversation between her and a man she had met only minutes earlier was actually taking place. 'Well,' she breathed thoughtfully, 'you've told me what you would be getting out of such a marriage—another shipping company, presumably greater wealth, a dutiful mother to your sister's children and the continuing freedom to sleep with whomever you like. That's a lot.'

Leo surveyed her with dark golden eyes and slowly smiled, his chiselled dark features more appealing than ever. 'It is…'

'I can see why the arrangement would appeal to you. But what would *I* be getting out of it?' Letty asked gently.

And she thought, *I'm not asking that—seriously I'm not. I can't possibly be considering such a crazy proposition from a man I don't even know! An unscrupulous, immoral man at that, one who prefers a mis-*

tress to a wife in his bed and makes no bones about it either! Absolutely and utterly shameless in his honesty.

Leo studied her, wishing he could read her better, but the smooth oval of her face was unrevealing. Indeed, they could have been discussing something as bland as the weather.

'Let me tell you the benefits of becoming my wife,' Leo urged in that husky accented drawl of his, which was both exotic and sensual.

CHAPTER TWO

'I DON'T KNOW how important money is to you,' Leo remarked deadpan.

'When you don't have money, but you need it, it's *very* important,' Letty countered with a toss of her head and a lift of her chin because she was telling the truth and didn't care if he judged her for it.

Leo rose from his seat and spread his lean brown hands in an expressive gesture that was wonderfully fluid. 'If you marry me, you will be able to have anything that you want. I am a very rich man,' he told her bluntly. 'I assume that you would want to organise private surgery for your mother and find a safer place for your family to live. You will also want the thugs, who are harassing your mother for payment of her loan, dealt with. Those are the difficulties that I can easily settle on your behalf. Only you can tell me what else you would want.'

Letty was astonished by how much he already knew about her life and her family's problems. 'Where did you get all that information? From Isidore?'

'From a very discreet investigation agency. I had to know exactly who you were before I could consider allowing you near the children,' Leo pointed out without a shade of remorse.

Annoyed by his invasion of her privacy and yet simultaneously understanding his reasons for doing so, Letty was bemused. 'And what did you think that you learned about me?' she prompted.

'That you put family loyalty over personal ambition and that no one you have worked with or studied with or enjoyed a friendship with has anything bad to say about you,' Leo recounted levelly. 'I was very impressed and immediately keen to meet you. Such fine qualities are rare.'

Not entirely untouched by that accolade, Letty coloured and watched him move restlessly across the room. He drew her eyes to him, no matter how hard she tried to look away. He had an intensity to him she had not met with in a man before. Leo Romanos was so much *more*. He emanated physical energy in an aura of power. A very strong character, a mover and shaker, a pretty dominant personality, but it would be a dominance laced with intelligence and control. Emotional, *very* emotional—she had seen that emotion flashing in his eyes when he'd referred to his late sister and the children in his care. When he was in a bad mood, she imagined people walked on eggshells around him. Women, she imagined, fell in the aisles around him, stunned by the raw sexual charisma he exuded.

And no, she was not impervious to his masculine appeal, she conceded ruefully. She doubted that many women were impervious to Leo and she was no different, her attention veering involuntarily to the pull of fabric across his long muscular thighs as he moved, the swell of his broad chest below his shirt as he breathed, the muscles there evident. Even fully clothed he was a disturbingly physical man, who would always attract attention and admiration.

'You talk about acquiring a wife much like you're shopping for a fine wine,' she commented quietly. 'It's not the same.'

'Isn't it? I can purchase the finest wine at the highest price and I still may not like the taste of it,' he fenced smoothly.

'I consider marriage to be,' Letty murmured levelly, 'a sacred bond between two people.'

'Yes, you are a practising Christian.' Leo acknowledged that detail, shifting his expressive hands again. 'But you are practical as well and you must know that sex causes a lot of grief in relationships. Take the sex out of the marriage and you have a working, reasonable partnership.'

'And an unfaithful husband,' Letty chipped in, again inwardly denying that she was having such a dialogue with him while wondering how she could possibly be intrigued by his attitude.

Leo shrugged a wide shoulder. 'Is that so important in the grand scheme of things? It's not as though you're in love with me. It's not even as though you know me.'

Letty's head was beginning to ache with the stress of the meeting to which she had walked in totally unprepared. She was too tired to think with clarity and her mind was increasingly awash with irrelevant but seductive images, such as her mother able to walk again, her brothers attending a less crowded and tough school and being able to eat what they liked, rather than what was cheapest. Lack of money, she registered unhappily, controlled their lives, limited it and removed all the choices. But the escape that Leo Romanos was offering carried risks as well.

'I've been up almost twenty-four hours,' Letty admitted. 'I need to sleep to process all this.'

Leo swung back to her, spectacular dark golden eyes locking to her. 'But you're *not* saying no out of hand,' he breathed with satisfaction.

'A drowning swimmer doesn't reject a lifebelt unless it comes anchored to a crocodile,' Letty responded wryly.

'I'm not a crocodile,' Leo told her.

'You have strong aggressive instincts,' Letty informed him.

'I am not violent…in *any* way,' Leo intoned, looking shaken that she might suspect otherwise.

'But who knows what damage you could do in other ways?' Letty fielded as she rose from her chair. 'Right now, I'm going home to bed.'

'You're too tired to bike it back,' Leo stated. 'I will have you driven home and one of my security team will return your motorbike for you.'

'I'm not into bossy men, Leo,' Letty warned him.

'I am considering your welfare,' he parried.

'My welfare is not your business.'

'Yet…'

'It's childish to always need to have the last word,' Letty said as she reached the door.

'So, that's why you're having it, is it?' Leo gibed, disconcerting her and pulling the door open for her with a smooth civility that she found equally surprising.

He escorted her all the way to the lift, the eyes of his employees swivelling in their direction. He stabbed the call button at the same time as he settled a business card into her hand. 'My number. Let me know if you're prepared to move forward with this. If you are, I will collect you on Saturday morning at ten and introduce you to the children,' he announced.

Letty turned exasperated eyes onto his chest and then tilted her head back to study his lean strong face and the resolve etched there. 'I don't know how I feel but there is only a one in ten chance that I will agree! I don't want to get married. I'm not ready to be a mother…and I *loathe* promiscuous men!'

'I would take issue with that word,' Leo framed, his strong jawline clenching hard. 'But we will not discuss that insult in a public place.'

Breathing in deep to prevent herself from snapping back at him, Letty stepped into the lift. 'Goodbye, Leo. It's been…interesting.'

The most bloody frustrating woman he had ever met! Leo strode back to his office, his brain buzzing at top speed. So stubborn, so rigid. How dare she label him promiscuous? He was not and never had been promiscuous. Yes, there had been many women in his bed over the years, but he was thirty-one years old and a certain level of experience was natural. He was prepared to concede that keeping a mistress was a little less common but he never stayed with the same woman for longer than three months and while she was in his life, the arrangement was exclusive. He hadn't had a one-night stand since he was a teenager and even then he hadn't slept around.

Isidore's granddaughter was fiercely intelligent though, not a woman to be pushed into a premature decision…but coaxed? Leo didn't know how to coax a woman because he had never had to make that much effort with a member of her sex, but he also knew that he had just met a woman he would be satisfied to call his wife. As far as he was concerned the deal was made and only the date needed to be set. She didn't have a choice, did she? Her life had been overwhelmed by family difficulties and, much as he admired her loyalty, it annoyed him that she had swerved from her own agenda and had allowed her mother's foolish decisions and misfortunes to restrict her.

Letty rode home and Leo need not have worried that exhaustion would make her a less than cautious rider. Leo had set off a chain reaction inside her head. Out of his presence, she could think again, see possibilities and spot the issues he had overlooked. What about *her* sex life? Was she expected to keep a male version of a mistress somewhere? Or was she supposed to cross her legs like the virgin she was and get by without sex?

In truth, Letty didn't know if she would ever want sex with a man. Being a high achiever had never helped her social life. The more she had shone at school, the fewer friends she'd had and she had been christened a nerd and a geek. University and competing with her peers had provided a different learning curve but no boyfriend had ever contrived to make Letty want more than kisses and companionship. All of them had wanted more from her than she was prepared to give because she had always put her studies first. She had once toyed with the idea of just having sex with someone purely to find out what it was like, but she wasn't sufficiently curious and was too cynical to expect fireworks from the experience, so she had retained her ignorance and her innocence.

A man like Leo, however, would have made her want more and would have incited her curiosity. She knew that instinctively and it made her wary of him. He made her feel vulnerable and she didn't like that either. He was too clever as well, too clever to be trusted. Had she had more respect for her grandfather, she would've asked his opinion of Leo Romanos but Isidore Livas was scarcely a disinterested observer and she could not put her faith in him. Presumably her grandfather wanted this alliance to go ahead and he was equally keen for Leo to become his heir. Letty had no doubt that Leo was a blazing success in the business world.

When she arrived home, her mother needed painkillers and she went back out again to collect the prescription. The painkillers were highly addictive and that worried her, for her mother had been on them for quite some time. While she was out, she bought food for dinner and when she returned for the second time her mother was standing rapt in front of the table, on which sat a gorgeous bouquet of flowers, delivered in a vase and ready for display.

'For you…' the older woman said with warm appreciation, turning to study her flushed daughter with curiosity. 'You've been keeping secrets. Who's Leo?'

Letty grabbed the card. It just said 'Leo', but that was all it needed to say.

'Leo?' she repeated, her mouth running dry. 'He's one of the residents' relatives at the care home,' she fibbed in desperation.

'Is he young?' Gillian pressed.

'Yes, and good-looking.'

'Well, don't freeze this one out, the way that you do when men show an interest in you,' her mother urged worriedly. 'Be nice to this one.'

'Mum, I'm only twenty-four. I've got plenty of time to meet someone. Stop worrying about me,' Letty said wryly, giving the older woman a hug. 'I'm off to bed.'

She had hoped to climb into bed and go out like a light but her mind had other ideas: visions of her mother restored to mobility and no longer reliant on painkillers, her family in a home in a decent area with furniture that wasn't worn and shabby and the boys clad in the sports gear of their dreams. Seductive images, she conceded ruefully, cursing Leo Romanos for tempting her before grabbing her laptop to look him up online.

The Greek billionaire, the shipping heir, consummate tycoon…giver of flowers, charming when he wanted to be.

Also a womaniser, she reminded herself, discovering a whole slew of images in which Leo appeared in company with various women but all of them were identikit brunettes. It seemed he had a type and his type was tall, curvy dark-haired women. Of what interest was that to her? Why was she even looking? Scolding herself, Letty returned to trying to sleep while attempting not to recall that Christmas was only just round the corner and that the coming festivities would be just as cheerless as the last.

Christmas was impossible to do on a strict budget and, what with the loan payments due every month and keeping up with the household bills, there was no room for treats or extras. Her brothers were still children and it was hard for them to do without what other boys their age took for granted. If she married Leo, a persuasive little voice whispered inside her head, she could give her family a fantastic Christmas. All their worries would disappear, wouldn't they?

Of course, *she* would be taking on a whole fresh set of worries, striving to meet Leo's high expectations of a wife and mother to four orphans, but if her family was happy and secure, did that really matter? She was good at coping with challenges, in fact the tougher a project was, the harder she worked to complete it. She did her best work under pressure...and Leo would put her under pressure, she had no doubt of that.

Letty pillowed her weary head on her hand and stretched out. Obviously, she would have to deliberate on his proposition because nothing more promising was likely to come her way. If she said no, she would be condemning her family and herself to their current lifestyle for the next few years, at least. That was depressing but it was a fact. Her moral scruples were in conflict with her practical nature. There were too many unknowns for her to reach a decision. What would happen when she wanted a child? Or *he* did? And how long was he expecting the marriage to last? And what about the medical studies she wanted to take up again?

That Thursday evening, thinking longingly of her approaching weekend off, Letty performed her usual round of the patients, checking who was settled, who might need the attentions of the doctor on call later on, while stopping to speak to regular visitors, who wanted information about their relatives or had requests to make. She returned to her office to take her break at eleven and on her path through the quiet reception area she was shaken to see Leo.

In the sleek cashmere overcoat and red silk scarf he wore over a dark suit teamed with a gold silk tie, he looked exactly like the legendary international business mogul he was. His dark carnal beauty flooded her with mesmerising force and momentarily she felt boneless and her knees wobbled, butterflies careening frantically in the pit of her stomach. Letty froze in reaction, disconcertingly aware of her hair in an unglamorous bun and the plain green nursing-type tunic and trousers she wore with a logo badge on her collar.

'Time for a break?' Leo murmured calmly. 'You look tired.'

'It's been a busy week,' she muttered, colliding warily with glittering dark golden eyes, her breath snagging in her throat.

'I have coffee and tea out in my car... You didn't phone,' he censured.

Her cheeks warmed and she gave a little shake of her shoulders, unsure what to say because she hadn't made her mind up yet and didn't want to admit that. In her own head she was a very decisive person but there were too many unknowns attached to Leo Romanos. 'I haven't made up my mind yet,' she admitted grudgingly.

'Then discuss your concerns with me over tea. It'll be very civilised and no doubt we can pretend we're not sitting in a car park,' Leo pointed out.

Letty went to inform her next in command that she was taking her break outside. A big black and unbelievably long and glossy limousine sat double parked.

'Why are you here?' she prompted as his driver

pulled open the door of the car for them and stood to attention as though they were royalty.

'I won't introduce you to the children unless I know you're planning to go ahead. I've never brought a woman home to meet them before and they've had enough upsets in their lives.'

Letty suppressed a sigh as he pressed a button and an incredibly well-stocked refreshment bar complete with refrigerator, hot water and china swung out. The limo was massive and the upholstery was palest pearl grey leather. Her seat was comfier than her bed and, keen to busy her restless hands, Letty selected a cup and a teabag from the wide variety available in a small drawer and added hot water.

'Would you like anything?' she enquired politely.

'No. I've just had dinner,' he responded with an impatient sigh.

Letty sipped her Earl Grey tea and reluctantly glanced at him, encountering the devastating eyes that she would've preferred to avoid, hating his effect on her. He was a force of nature, his temperament lava-hot and dangerous. 'I've spotted four major stumbling blocks to your proposition,' she admitted, her heart suffering a sudden thud as he tensed and his stunning golden eyes narrowed.

'*Four?*' he stressed in disbelief.

'Yes, you really haven't thought this marriage idea through thoroughly enough,' Letty informed him gently. 'What happens when you decide you would like a child?'

'I've already got four of them. That's not going to happen at any time in the near future,' Leo contended dismissively.

'Unfortunately, I don't have as big a window of fertility as you will have,' Letty pointed out quietly. 'I am likely to want a child of my own some time in the next ten years. I don't want to leave it too long and risk missing my chance to become a mother.'

Leo frowned, level black brows pleating. 'So, we use a laboratory and give you what you want when you want. I don't see a problem.'

Letty noted that he wasn't suggesting that they consider sex for her to conceive, not that she would've agreed to that while he was sleeping with other women, but it really bothered her to recognise the faint sense of disappointment rising inside her. Disappointment allied with curiosity, she acknowledged ruefully. He made her curious in a treacherous way. Letty was not in the habit of looking at a man and thinking of sex but Leo made her think of sex, wonder what it would be like, wonder what it would be like *with him*. And in that thought progression lay one very good reason why she shouldn't marry Leo Romanos.

Her breasts were peaking inside her bra, her thighs pressing together in reaction to the dull ache that was infiltrating her. She couldn't possibly marry a man who awakened her long dormant sensuality but who planned to break his marital vows on a weekly basis, for all she knew even on a daily basis. It would be a recipe for low self-esteem and unhappiness because she would feel rejected.

'That's two stumbling blocks dealt with,' Leo proclaimed briskly. 'What are the other two?'

'As soon as possible I would like to return to studying medicine,' Letty admitted.

'Why not? When I told you that I wanted a wife to

be a mother to my sister's children, I didn't mean to suggest that I expected you to become a stay-at-home wife. I employ an ample staff to take care of the children on a day-to-day basis. You would be free to return to your studies,' he assured her levelly. 'I am not an unreasonable man, Juliet.'

'Don't call me that... I've always been Letty.'

'I don't like the name,' Leo declared calmly. 'To me, you will always be Juliet and I don't know how it ever got shortened into something as ugly as Letty.'

'My mother called my father, Julian, Jules and, although she named me for him, she could never stand to call me Juliet because it made her think of him. That's how I became Letty.'

'But you're not a Letty, you're a Juliet,' Leo told her stubbornly.

Letty shrugged a shoulder in dismissal. She had no intention of changing her name back to please him. Having drunk her tea, she set the cup back tidily on the cabinet top. 'I have to get back to work.'

'You still haven't told me the fourth stumbling block,' Leo protested, dark glittering eyes full of frustration pinned to her.

'My sex life,' Letty said bluntly, abhorring the heat she could feel warming her cheeks.

'Your...sex life?' Leo demanded as if those two words were an incompatible combination. 'You won't have one, unless it's with me.'

In the act of climbing out of the car, Letty came to a sudden halt and scornful green eyes slammed back into his. 'That won't be happening as long as you have other interests in your life,' she assured him tartly. 'And while I'm not currently in a hurry to have a sex life, I imagine the time will come when I feel differently.'

Leo was transfixed. It was a major obstacle and he hadn't foreseen it. In fact, he had been so wrapped up in his own selfish desire to maintain his usual lifestyle and boundaries that he had utterly ignored the obvious. Obviously, Juliet would have the same needs as he did. He wasn't one of those outdated men who believed that women had a smaller appetite for the physical pleasures of life. But the thought of *his* wife getting into bed with another man, the thought of another man touching and enjoying what Leo instinctively saw as *his* property alone, genuinely appalled him. He paled below his bronzed skin. It was hypocrisy, complete hypocrisy, and he knew it and sealed his wide sensual mouth closed before he said something he knew he should not say. That feat of control established, he breathed again.

'We'll discuss that on Saturday,' Leo informed her with finality, knowing he had less than forty-eight hours in which to come up with a miraculous alternative that would prevent her from seeking sexual satisfaction outside their marriage.

'I thought you might say that,' Letty confided, a wry little smile curving her generous mouth. 'I can't believe you didn't think of that angle.'

And with that final mocking little sally, Letty walked back into the nursing home, her head held high while Leo tried to work out how the hell she had contrived to become the very first woman to turn the tables on him.

CHAPTER THREE

ON THE SATURDAY MORNING, Leo travelled up in the smelly lift of the tower block. It was not a salubrious experience but meeting his future bride's family as soon as possible was essential to the smooth running of his plans. He had dressed down for the occasion in jeans, deeming that appropriate attire for informal weekend wear and children, even though he rarely wore casual clothing.

Letty was stunned when the knock on the door disclosed Leo himself because she had been expecting his chauffeur or one of the bodyguards she had seen hovering at a discreet distance in the care home car park to come upstairs and collect her. And there he stood, all sleek and dark and sophisticated in a cashmere sweater in a soft oatmeal shade that accentuated his bronzed skin tone, designer jeans outlining his long powerful legs and narrow hips, teamed with the less subtle hint of a slim eye-wateringly expensive watch at a masculine wrist which suggested that he came from a class of society far removed from her own.

'Leo!' she heard herself say abruptly, taut with disconcertion and discomfiture at being faced with him sooner than she had expected.

'I believe it's time that I met your family,' Leo told her smoothly.

Letty froze, further taken aback, faint colour running up into her cheeks. 'Er... I...'

'Not something we can avoid,' Leo declared, cool and outrageously serene at the prospect.

It made Letty wonder what it took to unnerve Leo Romanos and once she found out she knew she would use it against him in punishment.

And little more than two minutes later he was dominating their tiny living room with his broad-shouldered height and positive buckets of charm. He accepted a cup of black coffee and engaged her mother in conversation. He came up with an entirely fictitious old lady whom he supposedly visited at the care home from time to time, a former employee of his father's who had been kind to him as a boy.

'Letty... I thought *you* said that Leo was related to...'

'Your daughter and I kept on bumping into each other in the corridor late at night. She doesn't always listen well,' Leo proclaimed forgivingly.

Dear heaven, he could act, and he lied like a trooper without a soupçon of evasiveness or unease, Letty registered in consternation, seeing that she would have to sharpen her skills to have any hope of ever outwitting Leo. And that quickly she appreciated that she was already thinking as though she was planning to marry him and that shook her because so many of her misgivings had still to be settled and she wasn't a woman who acted on impulse.

It had been years since she had seen her mother smile so much and he'd even coaxed some attention out of her brothers by showing them a nifty trick with the video game they were engaged in continuing to play in spite of their mother's strictures.

Leo perused his bride-to-be in the lift. She was the right type: he could feel it in his bones even though she was not at all the kind of wife he had once dimly envisaged. Clad only in worn jeans and a black rollneck sweater, she still somehow contrived to hold his attention. Her hair was braided at the front and long and loose at the back, tiny tendrils curling round her classic oval face, those wide sea-green eyes welded warily to him. There was no flesh on show and he wasn't used to that. He was accustomed to seeing everything a woman had to offer at a glance and inexplicably that covered-up look of hers, that modest mode of dress inflamed him. It made him look closer and turn away slightly from her as the hum of unwelcome arousal pulsed at his groin.

The full sweep of her breasts and the curvaceous swell of her derrière still swam before his inner eye and that lingering image vexed him. He didn't fantasise, he didn't *imagine* women naked. That was a teenage boy trait or the mark of an unsuccessful lover and even as a boy Leo had been skilled at getting what he wanted from the opposite sex. He didn't have to fantasise; he generally only had to show interest in a woman to know that satisfaction would be easily obtained. Yet one glance at Juliet in any garb and he was speared by sheer lust, wanting to touch, wanting to taste, wanting to ride to satisfaction between those slender thighs.

And yet she was the *one* woman whom he should be determined not to take. But maybe that was the secret of her appeal, he reasoned in frustration—the knowledge that she was out of bounds and forbidden. Maybe sex had become too easy, too available to fully engage his libido. Maybe what he really needed was some sort of diversion to direct his energy elsewhere. Clearly his current mistress was past her sell-by date and no longer able to attract him. That was what was wrong with him, he decided in a stark burst of relief; he had simply got bored with the current woman in his bed.

Letty barely breathed in the lift because the edgy atmosphere unsettled her. She focused on the dark shadow of stubble outlining Leo's strong jaw, the clenching of the muscles there, the sheer tension he emanated. Her breasts expanded as she snatched in a shuddering breath and stepped out into the foyer. The lace of her bra chafed her nipples and, as Leo clamped a guiding hand to her spine to urge her out of the building, she was engulfed in a wave of his scent, an achingly appealing medley of designer cologne and raw masculinity. Instantly, she stiffened, aware of the spurt of heat low in her pelvis and the uncomfortably damp sensation that followed. Annoyed that her body was betraying her with reactions she didn't want, she gritted her teeth. She couldn't afford to be attracted to Leo. It would be like walking through a minefield without any form of protection and she would be setting herself up for emotional damage.

After all, nobody knew better than Letty what it was like for a woman to love an unfaithful man. She had watched her mother with her stepfather, standing on the sidelines while Gillian suppressed her suspicions and accepted her husband's lies when he was late home or when phone calls came he couldn't explain or which he wouldn't answer around his family. The lies and evasions had been endless, and her mother had *wanted* to believe the lies because she loved Robbie and she hadn't wanted to credit the ugly truth that he had other women in his life.

But it wouldn't be like that with Leo, a cool inner voice reminded her soothingly. Leo wasn't prepared to lie. Leo preferred to be open and honest about his sexual preferences. He thought sex caused a lot of grief in marriage and that unusual outlook made Letty wonder how he had grown up and what his parents' relationship had been like. What experiences had taught Leo to think that way? Certainly, he didn't associate sex with the warmer emotions. It might even be true that he preferred sex without emotion getting involved at all, she reasoned. The more she thought about what motivated Leo, the more annoyed she became with herself for wondering and questioning everything about him as though he were some source of fascination. Of interest certainly, not fascination, she assured herself circumspectly. She wasn't that much of an idiot, was she?

'You're a very good liar,' she remarked in a brittle voice as the limousine drove off.

'We have to roll out an acceptable back story for your family's sake,' Leo fielded without skipping a beat. 'Unless, of course, you plan to tell them the truth—that you're only prepared to marry me for my money?'

In receipt of that stinging challenge, Letty shot him an outraged glance, green eyes sparking fire. 'Of course I'm not going to tell them that! It would break my mother's heart if she knew how I'm thinking and feeling right at this moment!'

'So, we're fortunate that I'm a good dissembler then,' Leo responded with satisfaction. 'But you need to work on being more convincing. At this point, a few lovelorn glances in my direction would be a good idea.'

'I don't *do* lovelorn!' Letty snapped, wanting to slap him hard enough for that teasing smile to die on his lips. 'I mean, why would I?'

'Because we don't have time to waste on a long engagement. I want the wedding to take place as soon as possible.'

'But I haven't agreed.'

'You're on the brink. You don't have any other options and you know that our marriage makes sense,' Leo countered with infuriating conviction.

Letty didn't appreciate the reminder that she had no other options. She felt as though she had tried to spread her wings, only for him to drag her cruelly back to solid earth again. Unfortunately, he was right: she was going to marry a man she didn't know on terms that appalled her because, from what she knew, the good that that marriage would bring far outweighed the bad. She could help her family and, in so doing, pay back some of the loving support and encouragement she had received from them over the years. And hadn't she long understood that most major gains in life entailed major sacrifices as well?

'I'm still thinking it over,' Letty fielded, her cheeks pink with annoyance, her eyes bright as she encountered dark golden eyes fringed with spiky black lashes that remained resolutely unimpressed by her stubborn response.

Mercifully the car was already pulling in to park. She gazed out at the frontage of the most magnificent mansion she had ever seen outside a movie. Her eyes wide, it felt entirely normal to stare at the rows of gleaming windows and the porticoed entrance which once would have sheltered guests climbing out of carriages drawn by horses. '*This* is where you live...or was this your sister's house?' she queried.

'It's mine. I sold my sister's townhouse and stored the contents.'

'That must've been disruptive for the children...to lose their home and their parents at pretty much the same time.'

Leo sighed, long brown fingers flexing as he spread his hands. 'I'm not a saint. I've given up a lot, but I wasn't prepared to give up my home as well. There's a lot more space here too and four kids and a bunch of nannies take up an enormous amount of space. My sister didn't have nannies. She was a devoted mother, determined to do everything herself.'

'She was younger than you...right?'

'Five years younger. Our mother died bringing her into the world,' Leo confided. 'Although my father remarried soon afterwards, we didn't have a happy family life as children. Ana met her husband, Ben, young and they were both crazy about kids. A large contented family was Ana's dream.'

Letty picked up on the slight hoarseness of his voice. He had loved his sister and he missed her, regretting that the younger woman had not survived to live her dream.

'I'm doing my best with Ana's kids but it's not working out well,' Leo admitted stiffly.

'It's only been six months since they lost their parents. It takes a long time for a wound like that to heal,'

Letty said gently as she slid out of the car, suddenly feeling seriously *under*dressed for her grand surroundings.

The hall was huge, with a marble floor and a grand staircase with a wrought iron balustrade. A massive painting dominated the landing, a portrait of a beautiful smiling brunette. Leo urged her into a drawing room that was so opulent it took her breath away. The décor was country house stylish with wallpaper that looked hand-painted, capacious velvet sofas and a massive fireplace but there was a definite contemporary edge to the sculpture in the window embrasure and the glass tables. Absolutely no allowance had been made in the room for a family with young children, she realised wryly. It was an elegant showpiece room for adults and had the air of a space rarely used.

'Unc' Leo!' a childish voice trilled.

Letty spun in time to see a small dark-haired child break free of a uniformed nanny's hold and rush across the room to embrace Leo's legs.

'Letty, this is Popi,' Leo announced as a smaller child bounded over to greet him, another little girl in a princess net outfit. 'And this little minx is Sybella.'

The other nanny settled the baby in her arms down on the carpet with some toys and the little boy tugged his hand loose of hers and moved closer.

'Cosmo!' Popi hissed, grabbing his hand as she moved over to station him and herself behind her baby brother.

'Cosmo and Theon,' Leo completed with a frown as he dismissed the hovering pair of nannies with a quiet word.

Letty absorbed Popi's defensive stance with her siblings and understood. As the eldest, Popi had taken on the role of protecting her younger siblings and Letty was perceived as a threat. She went down on her knees in front of the baby, who gave her the most adorable wide gummy smile of welcome, unaffected by his sister's disapproval. He held up his arms to be lifted and Letty couldn't resist the invitation, but she was very much aware of Popi's dismay.

'I'll just sit here,' she promised, gathering up Theon and settling into a seat beside the little girl. 'You stay close in case he wants you.'

'He won't. He's just a baby. He doesn't even know who you are,' Popi fired back at her, unhappy at her baby brother's friendliness.

'*Popi...*' Leo's intervention was clipped and cool and the little girl stiffened and dropped her head. 'What did we talk about over breakfast?'

'It's fine,' Letty interposed gently. 'Change is always threatening.'

'I don't want a new mother,' Popi whispered chokily.

'I'm Letty and you can call me that. Nobody can take the place of your mother,' Letty said softly, shooting Leo a warning glance when his lips parted as though he was on the brink of firmly disagreeing with that statement. 'But I do hope that when you get to know me we can be friends.'

'I have lots of friends,' Popi told her.

'It never hurts to have one more,' Letty contended calmly as Theon clutched at her and went in for a kiss. She kissed him back, looked into his big dark trusting eyes and felt her heart literally thump because he was adorable.

Cosmo sidled over and leant back against her knee

while he ran a plastic car over the arm of her chair. He ignored Popi's calls to return to her side. Sybella clutched at Leo's jeans and then ran over to twirl in her princess dress and be admired. Popi stood alone, frozen in the centre of the rug, and her expression of loss and anxiety almost broke Letty's heart.

'Would you like to show me your bedrooms?' Letty asked, eager to leave that awkward moment behind as she stood up, cradling Theon on her hip. The minute the baby laid eyes on his uncle, he lifted his arms out and lurched in his direction instead.

'Show you toys…' Sybella offered, dancing and hopping on one leg like a tiny brightly coloured flamingo.

Upstairs they went, with Popi trailing reluctantly in their wake. Letty now understood Leo's concern about his sister's children. Popi was so busy trying to parent and protect her siblings that she couldn't relax and simply be a child. It was equally obvious that Leo was the children's place of safety, but possibly he wasn't around enough to make them feel secure.

Letty strolled through a set of superb bedrooms crammed with toys. She was taken aback to note that even in Popi's room there were no photographs of the children's late parents and she mentioned that oversight in surprise to Leo.

'I thought it was kinder not to remind them but there'll be photo albums in the stuff I put into storage,' he replied.

'I think they should all have a photo. I also think that if you have a bedroom large enough and could bear the disruption,' Letty whispered, 'they could all sleep in the same room…just for a little while. I think it would help Popi relax more.'

It was a simple suggestion and not one Leo had considered. He hoisted his niece into his arms and asked her if she would like to share a room with her sister.

Popi beamed. 'Oh, yes, it would be just like home then...'

'You used to share with Sybella,' he recalled.

'Yes, but here in *this* house I'd like the boys too... I need to look after them,' Popi told him, silencing Leo with that assurance.

Watching Juliet adjust the gauzy wings on Sybella's fairy outfit and seeing the toddler come running back with a necklace she wanted to put on as well, however, Leo was content. He had brought the baby whisperer home, a kind and practical woman who would take the time and effort to work out what would make the children feel happy and safe in his house.

Lunch was served in a grand dining room. The same nannies appeared beforehand to whisk the children away. Evidently the children did not share their uncle's meals.

'For a first meeting that went very well,' Leo proclaimed with satisfaction as the first course was delivered. His black hair was ruffled by Theon's clutching hands, his stubborn jawline darkly stubbled, outlining the surprisingly full outline of his wide sensual mouth. As Letty looked, a tightness across her chest and butterflies dancing in her stomach, Leo glanced up, spearing her with narrowed dark golden eyes enhanced by thick black lashes. Those eyes were stunning, strikingly compelling, and heat flamed through her body without warning. She had to drop her attention back to her plate to gather herself again.

'It'll take time for the children to get to know and

trust me,' she pointed out, trying not to openly sali-
vate at the sight of the tiny savoury tart and salad on
the plate in front of her. 'Don't set the bar too high.'

'Unlike the nannies, who have come and gone, for
most of them don't want the responsibility of *four*
charges,' Leo stated wryly, 'you will be a constant
in the children's lives and that security is what they
need most.'

It struck her that she had already given unspoken
agreement to the marriage he had suggested and that
shook her. That wasn't how she operated. Even so, the
children had touched her heart and Leo had already
gone ahead and informed them that she was his intended wife. Consequently, backing out now wasn't really a viable prospect, particularly when Leo had boldly
reminded her that he was her *only* option. *Suck it up*,
she urged herself impatiently. By marrying Leo, she
could put her family's life back on track and, eventually, she would be able to return to studying medicine.
In any case, how could she possibly refuse an offer
that would put her mother back on her own two feet?

'All right, so I'm marrying you, but we still haven't
discussed that final stumbling block I raised at our last
meeting,' Letty reminded him resolutely. 'Going into
this, we both need to know exactly where we stand.'

Leo breathed in deep, knowing he couldn't afford to
tell her exactly how he felt about having a wife with a
sex life separate from his own, a wife who slept with
other men whenever she chose, an equal partner in
every way to himself. He had never contemplated taking a wife who would enjoy such freedom and he hon-
estly didn't think he could live with that concept. 'I

suggest that we play that by ear. Why do we have to have a game plan?'

'Rules agreed in advance ensure that things run more smoothly,' Letty told him.

'I'm more a spontaneous kind of guy,' Leo quipped. 'I don't believe that everything can be laid out in black and white before we even know what it will be like to share our lives.'

There was a certain amount of sense in that statement but Letty preferred rules. Rules, as she saw them, prevented misunderstandings and provided firm boundaries. 'I prefer black and white.'

'You're unlikely to get that with me,' Leo admitted simply.

'I disagree. I think you'll want a prenup and other safeguards before we marry,' Letty dared. 'Or am I wrong?'

Leo tensed, recognising that he was dealing with an astute woman. 'No, on that score you are correct. But financial arrangements fall into a very different category. Financial rules and safety measures are only common sense.'

Letty ate with appetite because everything on her plate was a treat. She told herself off for eating the dessert, reminding herself that she would have to work it off at the gym.

'Do you want your grandfather to stage and foot the bill for our wedding?' Leo enquired levelly over the coffee cups. 'He has already made that suggestion.'

Letty almost choked on her coffee. 'Has he indeed? Very generous of him, I'm sure!' she exclaimed, biting back further uncharitable words but only with difficulty. 'He wouldn't help us when we *really* needed his help, but if I'm doing what he wants suddenly he's ready to open his wallet. Sorry, that sounds bitter.'

'But understandable. I had to give you the choice, but I would prefer to organise everything for us,' Leo admitted quietly. 'Your grandfather would probably want to stage the wedding in Greece, which wouldn't suit either of us very well.'

A little embarrassed at having spoken so freely, Letty merely swallowed hard and nodded because travelling to Greece for a wedding certainly wouldn't suit her or her family. Her head was swimming a little from the awareness that she was discussing wedding arrangements with a man she had only met that week. It felt surreal.

'I will be inviting friends and business connections,' Leo declared. 'You, of course, will have your own guest list and I imagine your grandfather will also have names he wishes to put forward.'

'There won't be many on my list. We don't have any other near relatives living and only a few close friends worthy of an invitation.'

'What about your mother's parents?'

'They died years ago without ever having forgiven her for bringing me into the world,' Letty stated with a grimace. 'My maternal grandmother was in her forties when she had Mum and, like my grandfather, Mum's parents viewed my birth as a social embarrassment.'

'Thankfully, few are as judgemental these days,' Leo observed, reaching into his pocket to withdraw a small jewellery box and passing it to her without ceremony. 'It would please me if you wore this. In so far as it is possible for your family's benefit and that of the children, we should behave as though this is a regular relationship.'

Letty lifted the lid on a magnificent solitaire diamond ring and gasped in complete surprise. 'Gosh! You want me to wear an engagement ring?'

Leo lifted and dropped a shoulder as if to suggest that, regardless of his polite assurance that her wearing the ring would please him, he was, in fact, quite indifferent. 'I think your mother would appreciate the conventional touches, particularly when we are getting married so quickly.'

Letty slid the ring onto her finger, relieved that it fitted, her face warming with colour. 'How soon do you expect the wedding to take place?' she asked apprehensively.

'Within a couple of weeks.'

Letty was aghast at that short time frame. *'But—'*

'Now that we've agreed on how to move forward, why would we waste time?' Leo incised. 'I would appreciate it if you tried to spend some time with the children between now and then.'

'Of course. I only have to give a week's notice at work,' Letty mumbled, flustered by the fast pace of events and feeling more than a little overwhelmed by the prospect of marrying Leo, even though it wouldn't be a normal marriage, no matter how hard they tried to pretend otherwise.

'I'll organise a list of surgeons for you so that you can have your mother booked in for the procedure she requires. I would also suggest that you look at a list of properties I have available to choose accommodation that would suit your mother and brothers better than your current home,' Leo added. 'My lawyers will contact you with regard to the legalities of our agreement. Unfortunately, I'll be in Greece over the next few days handling the amalgamation of your grandfather's company with mine. If you need to contact me, you have my number.'

Letty breathed in deep and slow to steady herself. All of a sudden she was seeing that her world was about to be turned inside out and that while the end result might be a great improvement, it would also be even more challenging than she had expected.

'Er… I hate to mention it,' she muttered uncomfortably as she considered her family's most pressing problem and the state of sleepless anxiety that same problem kept her mother in. 'That loan—'

Leo studied her, dark golden eyes hardening to a bright diamond glitter. 'That will be dealt with *without* your input. It will be settled, and those men will never bother you or your family again,' he swore. 'You will also have a security team protecting you from now on.'

'For goodness' sake!' Letty began in disbelief.

'And a car and driver to take you wherever you want to go,' Leo completed as if she hadn't spoken. 'I want you to be safe. I don't want to take the risk of anything happening to you. On our wedding day you will become my wife and Isidore Livas's heiress and such precautions are, sadly, necessary in the world that we live in.'

'I disagree,' Letty protested.

'You don't have to agree with me. As of today, I am taking full responsibility for your safety and that of your family. You will no longer need to keep a cricket bat behind the front door,' Leo informed her grimly. 'Anyone who threatens you now will have *me* to deal with!'

'Careful, Leo,' Letty murmured after she had got her breath back, her eyes colliding with his shimmering angry appraisal. 'Your crocodile instincts are showing…'

Leo expelled his breath in a hiss. 'The sight of that cricket bat incensed me,' he admitted grudgingly. 'I will not have you living in fear any longer.'

CHAPTER FOUR

'HE'S A LITTLE like a magician,' Gillian Harbison contended as she looked out dreamily at the little garden of the ground floor apartment she had moved into the day before. 'Leo, I mean. He just waves his magic wand and suddenly your wildest dreams come true.'

'That's Leo.' Letty studied her mother, seated in her wheelchair by the patio doors that led out into the garden. The lines of stress and tension had eased on the older woman's face. She was booked in for surgery at a private clinic the day after the wedding. Her sons would be staying with their father until she was back on her feet again and her best friend was moving in with her to support her during her recovery. The bright modern flat with three bedrooms and more space than Gillian had enjoyed in years was simply the icing on the cake. It was the moment when Letty accepted that any sacrifice had to be worthwhile when it made her nearest and dearest so much happier.

That was why she had bitten her tongue and surrendered to almost every demand that Leo had made of her. Accepting his generosity without complaint or protest, not to mention his insistence on security precautions, was a key challenge for her independent soul but seeing her family blossom in response was her reward. Furthermore, she couldn't pretend to be a loving bride and fight with Leo at the same time, particularly when she was currently only able to fight with him on the phone, for Leo had been in Greece longer than he had expected. He had uncovered suspect financial practices in her grandfather's company that required his immediate attention.

Letty had visited the children every day since Leo's departure. She would go over in the afternoon, share an evening meal with them and then stay until bedtime. The night before, Popi had given her a hug after she had read her and Sybella a bedtime story. Slowly but surely the barriers were coming down as Letty became more familiar to the children. Since she had handed in her notice at work she had been incredibly busy, dealing with the wedding planner, shopping for a wedding gown and coordinating the million and one things that she now had to do. That had included searching for outfits for the children to wear at the wedding and dealing politely but firmly with her grandfather's demand that *he* play a bigger part in the ceremony. Isidore Livas had been keen to walk her down the aisle but Letty's mother was fulfilling that role in her wheelchair, having already confided that it would be the proudest moment of her life.

'So, what are you wearing for the hen do tonight?' Gillian asked with a smile.

Letty hadn't wanted a hen party, but her friends and former work colleagues did and it had felt mean to deny them the chance of a good night out because once she had mentioned her plans to Leo, he hadn't scrupled to organise that for her as well. He had ob-

tained entry for all of them to a VIP section in an exclusive nightclub where their entertainment and their
drinks would be free and, much as Letty had resented
him taking over, she hadn't had the heart to rain on
everyone else's parade.

'We're all wearing denim shorts,' Letty revealed
with a grimace. 'I haven't worn shorts since the summer before university and I had to buy a new pair because I've expanded since then. We'll freeze.'

'Not with a limo ferrying you round,' her mother
said quietly. 'Letty…you're only young once. Enjoy it.
You don't get a rerun when you realise what you've
missed out on. Go out and have a good time tonight
with your friends.'

'I will. I promise.' Letty bent down to hug the older
woman, annoyed that she had put a troubled furrow
between her brows.

'You are so lucky to have found Leo. I couldn't be
happier for you,' Gillian confided. 'He takes such an
interest in all of us. I just don't understand why you
haven't already moved into his home… I mean, you're
trekking back and forth to his house every day and I
can manage fine on my own.'

Letty had coloured at her mother's natural assumption that she was already sleeping with Leo. 'Leo and
I will be together soon enough… It's only forty-eight
hours until the wedding,' she pointed out.

'And you *do* love him, don't you?' Gillian pressed
anxiously. 'His wealth and those looks of his haven't
turned your head too much? Because neither of those
things will keep you together if you don't love him.'

'Mum… I realise that I'm not the world's most de-
monstrative person but believe me,' Letty urged with

as much conviction as she could muster. 'I *love* him! It was practically love at first sight.'

Lust at first sight, she adjusted with an inner wince of embarrassment as she dried her hair in the new bedroom that would only be hers until the wedding. She hated lying to her mother, but she didn't have a choice. And she felt guilty because she wasn't seeing the children that evening. The chaos of moving to a new apartment and the hen party organised for the same night hadn't left her a moment to call her own, even though Leo had sent professional house movers to smooth the way. The sheer speed at which Leo accomplished things still shook her.

Money talked, she thought ruefully—money *definitely* talked. Her grandfather had been positively warm when he called to congratulate her on her decision to marry Leo. He was elated at the prospect of his retirement from business, although, from a couple of stray comments he had made, she also suspected that he regretted that Letty, rather than his adored daughter, her Aunt Elexis, was to be the bride.

Letty rarely touched alcohol. When tensions were high in her mother and stepfather's marriage, Robbie had resorted to drink and the scenes and arguments that had resulted had put Letty off alcohol. At least her stepfather had never been violent, she conceded, seated with her friends and feeling ridiculous in her fake tiara and bridal sash. In truth she felt like the spectre at the feast. Her companions were having a whale of a time, but Letty was much too conscious that she wasn't a *true* bride on the brink of marrying a man that she loved and it not only made her sad but also made her thoroughly irritated with her oversensitivity.

In response, she decided to have a few drinks and within an hour she was contriving to laugh naturally at the silly sex jokes that usually made her stiffen up, painfully aware of her own ignorance in practice. An hour after that, she was game for taking a turn on the pole on the podium, following the example of her two university friends, who were better at letting their hair down than she was. The three of them had attended pole-dancing classes for several years, relishing the strength, skill and flexibility they had gained from the experience.

Leo was travelling home from the airport when Darius phoned him. He had grown up with Darius, whose father had been *his* father's bodyguard, and there was no one he trusted more to look after Letty. Yes, he had given way on the name because she refused to answer to Julie or Juliet or any other diminutive. And her opposition on that score had intrigued him because women rarely challenged Leo and, once he had got to know Letty, her name had mysteriously grown to fit her.

'How's the party going?' Leo enquired with amusement against the backdrop of loud thumping music.

'Your bride is having a blast,' Darius replied. She's waiting her turn to pole-dance. I tried to head her off because it's a little too public here but she's…well, she's her own woman.'

Leo came off the phone, struggling to even picture Letty on a pole. At worst she would hurt herself, at best she would embarrass herself. He groaned out loud and raked an impatient hand through his black cropped hair. He had assumed she was too sensible to get involved in any kind of mischief and he most certainly didn't want her photographed for posterity doing anything that would mortify her in daylight. Without hesitation, he told his driver to head to the club. 'She's her own woman,' Darius had said tactfully, meaning that Letty was as stubborn as a mule and had dismissed his attempt to dissuade her.

Theos. Well, she wasn't going to dismiss him as easily, Leo reflected with resolve, springing out of the car, leaving his own security team struggling to follow him at the same speed. He strode through the club and up the stairs to the VIP section, with a hasty gesture dismissing the manager who came running to attend him. It was *his* club and he knew it like the back of his hand. Unlike his father and Isidore, Leo had diversified, refusing to rely on shipping as his sole means of profit and that more liberal approach to business had served him well in the entertainment industry, in the hotel trade and in property development.

At the top of the stairs, only vaguely aware of Darius approaching him, Leo came to a sudden unrehearsed halt, transfixed by the sight of Letty spinning effortlessly round the pole, blonde mane of hair flying as she dipped and flipped upside down and then went off into a handspring that took his breath away.

Certainly, she wasn't going to embarrass herself, he conceded in shock, his attention locking to the tight denim defining her curvaceous hips and the extension of one long shapely leg that revealed a creamy stretch of inner thigh. Her chest heaved below the light top she wore, the firm swell of her breasts pushing against the fabric as she sucked in oxygen, her tiny waist and flat stomach revealed as the top lifted. It was the most erotic thing Leo had ever seen and there was nothing visually arousing that some woman somewhere, some time hadn't already treated him to.

'So, how are you planning to handle this diplomatically?' Darius prompted with unhidden curiosity.

'Like a caveman,' Leo admitted thickly, fighting the nagging pulse of arousal with the greatest difficulty because lust was surging through him in a volatile wave.

He strode through the crush, forcing everyone to yield to let him past, and pounced on Letty without hesitation. He lifted her before she could get a hold on the pole again and walked back to the table Darius indicated to sit down in the midst of the chattering women with Letty sprawled across his lap.

'I'm Leo,' he said cheerfully.

'This is a girls' night out,' one of the women told him tartly.

'Letty's tired,' Leo murmured, rearranging his bride like the floppy rag doll she resembled when her legs threatened to slide off him again.

'Leo…' Letty looked up at him with a sunny laid-back smile.

Letty wasn't tired: she was drunk.

'I'm taking you home.'

'Party pooper,' she mumbled, burying her face in his neck. 'You need a shave but gosh, you do smell amazing…'

Disconcerted, Leo grinned.

'Letty never drinks. We egged her on,' someone said.

'We wanted her to have fun.'

Leo gazed down at her, long brown fingers brushing her tousled hair off her brow. 'Did you have a good time?'

Letty made an admirable effort to sit up without the support of his arm. 'I had a fabulous time,' she told her companions with careful diction. 'Thank you all for coming.'

'I'm dizzy,' she complained on the stairs.

'Of course you are,' Leo assured her.

'I'm not drunk.'

'Only well-refreshed,' Leo incised.

'I don't want to go home like this.'

'I'm taking you home with me,' Leo told her smoothly. 'It's too late to phone your mother.'

'I'll text her. She won't sleep until I'm home or she's heard from me.' Letty sighed, pulling out her phone and discovering that she was all fingers and thumbs and that it was a battle to focus.

While she texted she swayed and Leo breathed in deep and slow. She was a vision, honey-blonde hair tangled and falling round her, crystal tiara lurching to one side, green eyes myopic in their intensity, her classic profile taut with concentration.

When she had finished, Leo scooped her off her feet and she exclaimed, 'I can walk perfectly well!'

'Not in those heels you can't,' Leo assured her as he settled her into the limousine, relieved that no paparazzi had been awaiting them outside. 'Imagine if you broke an ankle—'

'And then we couldn't get married!' Letty pointed out. 'Let me go back and break an ankle before we make the biggest mistake of our lives!'

'I don't make big mistakes,' Leo intoned, recognising the hint of panic in her wide gaze before stretching across her to grab the seat belt and secure it firmly around her, the fingers of one lean brown hand brushing against a slender thigh as he did so. 'All you're suffering from is an attack of cold feet.'

* * *

Letty shivered, goosebumps breaking out at that fleeting and entirely accidental touch. She looked up into smouldering dark golden eyes and her breath was held suspended in her throat for a long timeless moment. Close up, his eyes were stunning, an absolutely riveting mixture of tawny shades and those lashes made her weak at the knees. The portrait of the beautiful brunette on the landing in his house was of his late mother. The resemblance between mother and son was arresting, particularly around the eyes. She wondered what his father looked like because, having had a glimpse of Leo's mother, she wasn't at all surprised that Leo had the flawless beauty of a dark angel.

'Besides, I'd take you even with a broken ankle,' Leo told her huskily. 'Popi says you read much better stories than I do.'

'Sybella likes the same one over and over again but Popi needs more stimulation,' Letty muttered unevenly, oxygen seesawing in and out of her lungs as though she had been running because, that close to Leo's raw masculinity, she felt weak and breathless. 'And Cosmo only listens if you put pictures of cars or trains in front of him.'

Leo studied her flushed face, the languorous fresh green eyes welded to his, and he tensed and shifted in his seat, disturbingly aware of how aroused he was by her. The sight of her, so relaxed and confiding, was incredibly sexy. He was striving very hard not to relive those few staggering moments when he had seen her twirling round that pole with fluid grace and a sensuality that had taken him wholly by surprise.

'I'd listen if you were on that pole,' Leo muttered in a driven undertone. 'Sexiest show I ever saw.'

Letty frowned at him, her disapproval palpable. 'It was exercise, Leo. I went to classes for years and found it a great way of keeping fit and strong. It's not sexy, except to a certain type of man.'

'You *were* sexy,' Leo told her before she could christen him a pervert.

Her eyes widened because no man had ever given her that label before and it knocked her off balance. She had always been the sensible, practical one in her circle of friends, the one who looked after her mates and guarded the drinks and the handbags. She didn't know *how* to be sexy, had occasionally envied those to whom it came naturally but had ultimately decided that she was happier having her brains.

'*Incredibly* sexy,' Leo purred, threading a straying strand of hair back behind one small ear. 'But if you dance like that again in a public place…well, you won't like my reaction. I don't want other men perving over your body like that.'

Leo was so close that her head swam. Her throat tightened and her mind went blank and her chest heaved as she pulled in as deep a breath as she could manage. 'I don't think you should be saying that to me.'

Leo's hand came up to curve to her cheekbone. 'It's said. It was the truth. Don't argue with the truth.'

'But it sounded possessive, territorial,' Letty whispered in troubled rebuke.

'I'm not possessive,' Leo muttered thickly as his head lowered. 'But I probably am territorial. I can't change who I am to fit some perfect male blueprint.'

'Not asking, not expecting perfection,' she mumbled, mesmerised by the golden glitter of his eyes on hers and the trail of fireworks sparking off somewhere deep down inside her.

One hand wound into her hair to turn her face, the other curving to her spine to ease her closer.

And then his mouth came down on hers with a fierce lancing urgency that took Letty by storm. His tongue tangled with hers and it was as if every kiss she had ever dreamt of was being delivered all at once. He tasted of mint and brandy. With that first little taste, the power of his demanding mouth was on hers, pausing to stroke her lips wider apart and nibble seductively on the lower lip before invading the moist interior of her mouth for a second time. His explosive passion sent her spinning with her heartbeat thundering in her ears and her body flushing and heating in reaction. He was very passionate, teasing one moment, carnally sensual the next. Her fingers speared into his dark hair, delving into the thickness, marvelling at how silky it was.

Her other hand braced on a long muscular thigh to hold herself steady. She wanted more—for the first time ever with a man, she *wanted* more. A stampede of angry elephants wouldn't have dragged her out of Leo's powerful hold. Her fingers trailed down his neck and clawed into his jacket, her heart racing, the very blood in her veins on fire with a hunger that hurt. Every sensitive spot on her body seemed to ache and throb. In a sudden movement, she released her seat belt with jittery fingers and clambered clumsily over him, needing to be closer, needing that full body contact to settle her racing pulse.

Taken aback by that change in attitude from the most buttoned-up bride a man had probably ever contemplated marrying, Leo absolutely froze for a split second. He knew he couldn't do anything because only alcohol had released her inhibitions. He knew she would never forgive him if he took advantage of her. But he also knew that a rejection of any kind when she had made the first move would bury him deeper than Australia because he knew women. At the same time, he was fiercely aroused and sheet lightning couldn't have prevented the groan that escaped him when she ground down on him in a basic approach that was shockingly effective. As her pelvis pressed down on his, Leo was electrified by hunger.

'Leo…' Letty pronounced with distinct satisfaction as she studied him, pale soft hands cradling his cheekbones, fingertips gently smoothing the skin.

Leo thought she was waiting for him to do something, and he had sworn he would do nothing, so he was entirely unprepared for Letty to lean back where she perched on him and tug off her crop top, revealing the scorchingly lush swell of her breasts in an unexpectedly pretty embroidered bra. He had expected serviceable white cotton. A slight shudder ran through him as he contemplated those pale full mounds of flesh and he closed his hands to her hips in protest—hands somehow sliding down over those pert swells to flirt with the hem of her shorts. Shorts—Letty in short shorts—he thought in abstracted wonderment, fighting for the control he lacked.

'I thought you'd be all over me like a rash,' Letty confided hoarsely, big green eyes wide with surprise and innocence. 'I thought you were a player…but maybe *I just don't do it for you*.'

In desperation, Leo kissed her with urgent force and

she ground down on him again, dredging a grudging groan of appreciation from his wide muscular chest as his fingertips grazed the soft silky skin of her inner thighs in an attempt to hold her still and prevent her from teasing him further. The tip of a finger slid beneath the hem and learned the damp silky welcome of her there and a breathless moan parted her lips beneath his and Leo was lost in the magic of her response. In all his life Leo had never been in such a state of excitement over so little and his control broke.

Letty was in a heaven without boundaries, her body seduced and sensation seducing her. Nothing had ever felt so physically good to her before, no previous experience had ever lit her up like a star from the inside out. *He* was touching her and she liked it, dear heaven, she liked it, indeed *loved* how with every mesmerising skim of those clever fingers she shivered and shook on the edge of something she didn't know but had somehow always secretly craved. Her hips were moving of their own accord, little sounds brimming beneath the erotic pressure of his mouth still on hers. And then suddenly the pressure tightening in her pelvis became unbearable and she was flying sky-high and inwardly screaming from the sheer glory of sexual delight that engulfed her.

Well, now you've done it, a snide little voice announced to Leo inside his swimming head. He shifted Letty into a more comfortable position until a faint little snore that brought a grin to his taut mouth warned him that fate had taken care of the problem for him. He would put her to bed and say nothing, make his usual dawn start at the office and thereafter act as though nothing had happened. Ignore, ignore, he urged himself firmly. She had called him a player and, in terms of what he estimated to be her level of experience, perhaps she saw that as an apt label, even if it wasn't.

Leo was perplexed when he settled Letty down on a guest room bed and removed her shoes only, before spreading a quilt over her. What was it about her that turned him on so hard and fast? He behaved like a sex-starved teenager with Letty and, while it was true that he was currently between mistresses and without a woman in his life, no other woman had ever made him lose focus and control as he had in the car with her. Hunger and need had overwhelmed him and he didn't like it. In retrospect, he didn't like that *at all*. Leo was careful never to lose control, never to want a woman *too* much. He wouldn't risk falling in love with the wrong woman, as his father had with his vindictive stepmother, who had loathed Leo purely because he truly knew what a slut she was, one who had tried to climb into her stepson's bed when he was twenty-one…

Loving the wrong woman could blind a man to his family's needs and make him weak and treacherous. It had happened to Leo's father, Panos Romanos. He had married a much younger woman. Katrina had wed him only for his wealth and had never loved him back. That marriage had slowly but surely destroyed Leo's family. As soon as she could, his sister Ana had fled that unhappy background and married far too young, desperate to create a happy family life. Leo, less vulnerable than his sibling, had merely decided that sex and marriage should always remain separate entities. He didn't need to love a wife to be a good husband, he only needed to like and respect and care for her. But then, had it not been for Ana's four needy children, he might never have married at all, he acknowledged grimly.

Letty wakened with a splitting headache. A hangover, she registered in dismay, sitting up in bed and noticing the glass of water and the painkiller set on the cabinet beside her. She reached for both with a groan, her brain a swirl of tangled images. She had got on that pole in public, she recalled in dismay and embarrassment, and then she recalled kissing Leo…and more.

Dear heaven, in the grip of urges stronger and more primal than she had ever dreamt existed, she had flung herself at him like a nymphomaniac, she recalled in horror. She had an image of peeling off her crop top and throwing it. And she remembered every second of what had followed with shuddering accuracy. Her sense of humiliation was so intense that she moaned out loud with self-loathing. How could she have done that? How could she have behaved like that?

He had been aroused too. She shifted in the bed, a mortifying heat warming her pelvis at the knowledge that she had had that effect on him. But she needn't be feeling like some wildly sexy seductress, she censured herself bitterly. Just about any man would've been put in that state by what *she* had been doing. It was certainly not a compliment to her personal attractions, such as they were. She wanted to blame him for what had happened but knew it would be unfair when she had offered so much encouragement. She couldn't imagine how she would ever look Leo in the eye again, which wasn't good when it was their wedding day in less than twenty-four hours.

It was a huge relief to go downstairs in her embarrassing shorts and discover that Leo had left for the office hours before. Popi's giggles at her appearance were somehow healing, the little girl's innocence soothing, and by the time Letty had cuddled Theon, set Cosmo's cars out in a line for him and done Sybella's hair in a princess style adorned with the bridal tiara from the night before, Letty was well on the road to recovery and telling herself that she was too sensitive, too naïve...

Leo, however, was having a difficult morning. No matter how hard he tried to shut it out and regain his usual deep concentration, he kept on remembering the feel and look of Letty on his lap in the limo and the taste of her on his lips. He was fantasising about a woman he had sworn he would leave untouched, he acknowledged grimly. A woman who set him on fire. A woman who had broken down his disciplined barriers and subjected him to a long, hot, sleepless night craving what he couldn't have. He had chemistry with Letty to a level that inflamed him. But he was not ready to embrace anyone's *sacred bond*.

Those two words said it all to Leo. He was not and would never be a one-woman man. Look at what that obsession for Katrina, his stepmother, had done to his spineless father! It had brought his father low, blinding the older man to his beloved's flaws.

And while Leo agonised and regretted, with a series of curses that he was rarely driven to use because sexual frustration was new to him, the solution finally came and it was stunningly simple. His brain had thrown out the obvious answer.

He blinked, the lush black lashes that enthralled Letty shooting up, a glow of satisfaction and relief warming the tawny depths of his eyes… *Of course*—the only answer that made sound practical sense and it would surely appeal to Letty as much as it appealed to him.

CHAPTER FIVE

SEATED IN HER CHAIR, Gillian flipped open the jewellery box that had been delivered and gasped out loud. 'Oh, my word, Letty... Come here and see!'

Letty rustled over in her bridal gown and was almost blinded by the flashing white fire of the diamond tiara, earrings and necklace laid out in the wide velvet-lined box. She flipped up the note enclosed in the box, in which Leo informed her that the set had belonged to his mother and he would be pleased if she wore the pieces. 'A little extravagant for me,' she began uncertainly.

'Nonsense, this is going to be a big fancy wedding attended by a lot of well-heeled people,' her mother told her roundly. 'And when a man hands over the family heirlooms *before* the wedding, you say "Thank you very much indeed" and wear them!'

Letty reddened and lifted out the tiara to anchor it into the thick mass of her upswept hair. Unlike the fake one she had worn on her hen night, it fixed in with ease. Adorned in the diamonds, she studied herself in the mirror, her hands trembling a little as her fingers dropped from attaching the last earring. In truth she barely recognised herself. She had had her hair and make-up done earlier that day at a local salon but, because she didn't own a full-length mirror, she could only see herself from the waist up.

Even so, she still cherished the image she had seen when she'd picked her dress from the designer studio Leo had instructed the wedding planner to escort her to. It was a simply glorious dress and she had fallen for it before it had even been removed from the hanger. It reminded her of an Edwardian tea dress except it was much more finely tailored, the styling accentuating her small waist and smoothing over the generous breasts and hips she preferred to conceal. Except when you got the goods out for Leo, a snide little voice reminded her at the optimum wrong moment because she had been training herself very thoroughly to totally bury and disremember that little incident in the limousine.

After all, Leo had been around the block a few times and he was not innocent. Since she had not seen him since then, he evidently wanted to overlook that wanton little episode and so did she, so *forget*, she instructed herself impatiently. In terms of their agreement, what was a meaningless little kerfuffle in a car to do with anything?

The previous week, Letty had signed a prenuptial document that ran to many pages of impenetrable legalese. But she had read and digested and ensured that she understood every word of it because she wasn't the kind of woman who signed anything on trust. She had *agreed* that Leo's infidelity would not be grounds for a divorce and that clause had had a sobering effect on her because it etched his future betrayal in stone for her. No sacred bond on offer from Leo, she recalled cynically. If their marriage did break down, however, she would retain some access to the children and a financial settlement that ran to lottery win figures. Nothing whatsoever was being left to chance in their marriage. In addition, she would have to have a child fathered by Leo for her baby to qualify for the Romanos name and inheritance.

Literally tormented by nerves, Letty climbed out of the limousine, winter sunshine glittering over the beautiful beaded lace on her gown and firing up the diamonds. She had never felt so self-conscious in her life and only the sight of her mother and Jenna, her closest friend from university, waiting with the children in the church porch settled her down again.

Popi and Sybella were resplendent in dresses that matched the bridesmaid, Jenna's, the little girls twirling with pleasure in their floaty skirts and chattering while Cosmo, quite indifferent to his smart little outfit and any sense of occasion, was clambering all over a stone bench. Leo had been amazed that she wanted to include the children in the bridal party while Letty had seen their inclusion as a necessity. While Leo might be too empathetically dim to appreciate the fact that what they were really trying to achieve with their marriage was the creation of a *new* family to make his nieces and nephews feel secure, Letty was not.

The walk down the aisle in the big packed church full of staring strangers disturbed Letty because she was uncomfortable being the cynosure of attention. She kept her hand resting lightly on her mother's shoulder and focused on Leo, utterly, effortlessly and flawlessly gorgeous, awaiting her at the altar. If only it had been their *real* wedding, she found herself thinking and she flushed, hastily squashing that foolish notion, assuming that all the frilly trappings of the day were confus-

ing her. Certainly, Leo in a morning suit was a sight
to behold with his sleek dark angel beauty, his perfect features bronzed and composed, those dark eyes
steady and serious, not softened or bright with the love
he might have felt for a genuine bride. Inwardly, Letty
swore at the tenor of her thoughts.

'You look fantastic,' Leo told her as she reached
the altar.

Of course, he had to say something like that, it was
expected of him, and it was almost as if someone had
yelled 'Showtime!' in Letty's ear. She switched on her
approximation of a bright bridal smile because Leo
had made it clear that their agreement was private,
and the rest of the world were to be left to believe that
they were a normal couple. As if she would ever have
captured a guy with Leo's looks and wealth in the *real*
world, Letty found herself thinking with helpless cyni-
cism, reckoning that it was little wonder that people
were curious and staring while they wondered how she
had contrived such a miraculous feat.

The beautiful words of the ceremony were something she tried not to dwell on or feel even slightly bitter about because, all else aside, this was *not* how Letty
had once vaguely imagined her wedding day would
be: with a groom by her side who loved and cared for
her as she cared for him, a true partnership of hearts
and souls. She reminded herself sternly of the benefits
that the wedding had already brought to her family and
would bring to Leo's orphaned nieces and nephews. It
was foolish to crave some starry-eyed ideal, she told
herself firmly, because that craving was a fantasy—a
fantasy that Leo would definitely never deliver.

'*Diávolos...*' Leo whispered the curse in her ear as

they progressed back down the aisle. 'That's the worst bit over.'

Letty laughed. Yes, that sentiment was very much Leo. He had as much sensitivity as a brick thrown at a window. Airy, feminine, finer feelings about weddings were foreign to him. Cosmo clutched at her skirts and she bent down and lifted him up, pressing a kiss to his troubled little face. 'You don't like the crowds, do you?' she gathered, holding him close, enjoying the sweet baby smell he still retained.

'I warned you that this might be too much for them,' Leo declared.

'They need the memory of being part of this,' Letty told him gently and only then registered that she was having her first conversation with Leo since that shameful little episode in the limousine. Her face warmed but she buried the recollection deep again. She had been brazen and silly and she had embarrassed herself, but that was human and it would be pointless to punish herself about something she could not change.

Leo was hoisting Sybella to his shoulder when a tall, slender blonde in a blue dress approached them. 'What on earth are your nannies doing, Leo?' she demanded imperiously. 'The kids should be out of sight and out of mind at such an occasion.'

Reluctant to offend a stranger, Letty swallowed back a sharp retort.

'We *want* them with us today,' Leo stated smoothly in direct contradiction of his words to Letty only seconds earlier. 'Katrina, meet Letty… Letty, this is my father's wife, Katrina.'

Grateful then that she hadn't snapped out a tart response, Letty absorbed the reality that Leo's stepmother, Katrina, was much younger than she had expected and English into the bargain. She smiled.

But the pretty blonde wasn't even bothering to look her way. Indeed, all her attention, her curiously *avid* attention, was for Leo. 'I just can't believe the size of the sacrifice you're making for those kids...actually getting married,' she said in an incredulous tone. 'Your father and I were astonished.'

Katrina's very blue eyes were locked on Leo, her fascination with him so strong it was tangible. Dear heaven, his stepmother was in love with him, Letty registered with shocked distaste. Luckily the photographer wanted a few shots at that point and Katrina was forced to back off while the nannies reclaimed the children. In the crush around the porch steps she watched a white-haired older man with a hint of Leo's cast of feature join Katrina, undoubtedly his father.

'I didn't realise your stepmother was much closer to your age than your father's,' Letty admitted simply on the drive to the hotel where the reception was being staged.

Leo compressed his lips. 'She's fourteen years older than me. She was twenty when my father married her. I was six. Ana was a baby. After her arrival in our lives I don't have one good memory of my childhood. She doesn't like kids, but she wanted one of her own to cement her position in the family. When she failed to conceive, she resented Ana and me even more.'

'She doesn't resent you now,' Letty pointed out, not being a woman to ignore a controversial topic, in spite of the warning signs that Leo's harsh diction and grim expression put out. 'In fact I'd say she's in love with you.'

Leo's big shoulders tensed and his teeth gritted

but he said nothing, deeming it a topic better left untouched.

'No comment?' Letty looked at him in disbelief. 'I suggest that your stepmother is in love with you and you have nothing to say at all?'

'I wouldn't call it love,' Leo countered between clenched teeth, feeling that he had no choice other than to be honest about the situation since Letty was too astute to be fooled and left ignorant. 'Katrina began flirting with me when I was sixteen and by the time I was twenty-one she was trying to seduce me!'

'Oh, my goodness!' Letty exclaimed with shocked distaste, registering that she had had to pressure him to surrender that truth about his father's wife because naturally such a sordid secret must have put a huge burden on Leo. 'Did you tell your father?'

'Of course not… It would have destroyed him!' Leo framed harshly. 'He adores her. Whatever faults I have, I am at least loyal and I care about my father even though he has been pretty hopeless as a parent. Katrina, however, disgusts me.'

'I shouldn't have pried,' Letty muttered ruefully, watching the anger she had ignited fade from his taut, lean dark features while noting the pain he was striving to bury about his disturbing past. 'But I sort of felt I had to know the family background so that I didn't put my foot in it.'

'Don't worry. We won't see much of either of them. My father and Katrina live in New York,' Leo informed her. 'He's devoted to her. Whatever she wants, she gets. I remember a huge row many years ago about the diamond set you're wearing. Katrina wanted them but they belonged to my mother and her jewellery was left to her children in her will. Katrina couldn't get past the law.'

'Is that why I'm wearing it today?'

'Only one of the reasons. You're my wife. You're a Romanos now and you are entitled to wear my mother's diamonds.'

'You've never told me anything about your mother either,' Letty remarked.

'I have few memories of her. She died having Ana. In those days, we lived on her family's island... My mother was an heiress from a far wealthier family than my father,' Leo stated wryly. 'Ios, the island, now belongs to me, along with everything else that was my mother's. Her inheritance was protected by an unbreakable family trust. Katrina was not best pleased to marry my father and learn that he wasn't as rich a man as she had naively assumed.'

'Serves her right if that's all she cared about,' Letty said roundly.

'I've always believed that she was his mistress before she was his wife. My mother may have died before her time, but I suspect that if she had lived my father would have divorced her for Katrina because he was and still *is* besotted with her.'

'There must be a huge age gap between them.'

'Twenty-odd years.'

Letty raised a brow but knew that it worked for some couples even though it clearly hadn't worked for Leo's father and stepmother. 'I wonder if your mother knew your father had a mistress.'

Leo took the easy way out of that unanswerable question by shrugging a broad shoulder, but his expression was grim, belying that show of casual acceptance. 'It's how the marriages in my family have always worked. Marriage is for children, inheritance, property protection. It's got very little to do with sex.'

Letty blinked. 'Maybe for very rich people,' she qualified uneasily and then she finally wondered in dawning dismay if possibly he was into some sort of kink that the average wife was unlikely to deliver. That prospect hadn't occurred to her before but, the more she thought about it, the more she thought that to be a possible explanation for his instinctive mental separation of sex and marriage.

After all, there had to be some very good reason why he thought that way. Ancestors with mistresses being an accepted way of life for the men? The stepmother from hell? The stepmother who had been his father's mistress? An unrepentantly unfaithful father, who must have hurt his mother? Wasn't that a more probable truth? That Leo suffered from that clichéd view of women as either angels or whores? A belief system that had been born in the early death of his mother and the arrival of a shamelessly unscrupulous stepmother?

'I know you don't understand my attitude,' Leo commented, startling her with that perception. 'We'll discuss it over dinner tonight.'

Letty was disconcerted by that suggestion, not having expected Leo to be so open on such topics. Ironically, in spite of her curiosity, she was in no hurry to hear his views, preferring to stuff the whole thorny question of his marital infidelity under a large mental rock and leave it buried there. What she didn't know couldn't unsettle her, after all. Ignorance would be preferable.

They arrived at the hotel. Letty drank champagne, greeted a never-ending line of guests, exchanged pleasantries and smiled. Her aunt, Elexis, her grandfather's daughter, cornered Letty when she emerged from the cloakroom after a quick touch-up of her make-up. Elexis was as thin as a playing card and a very attractive woman with a chic blonde bob.

'You look very like photos I've seen of your father, Julian,' the blonde commented on the subject of her late half-brother. 'Did you ever even get to meet him?'

Letty chose to ignore the rather offensive tone of that question.

'Several times when I was a child. My mother had an on-off relationship with him in the early years, before she realised that he would never settle down and stay clean,' Letty admitted quietly. 'But he was her first love and it was hard for her to step away from him.'

'You sound like a romantic. Leo won't like that,' Isidore's daughter proclaimed.

Letty simply smiled. 'I believe that you're getting married in the spring,' she said, keen to change the subject because she felt a little awkward about the fact that Leo had, years earlier, considered marrying Elexis.

'Yes, I can't wait. Anatole adores me,' Elexis told her smugly. 'You see, *I* wanted more from Leo than he was willing to give me. I wanted fidelity and I know for a fact that he's not willing to pledge that.'

'How do you know?' Letty asked in as mild a tone as she could manage.

'His current mistress is a guest at your wedding… and *you* didn't know?' Elexis queried in unkind surprise. 'Mariana Santos—that's her over there with the lady in the lime-green hat. Mariana, Spain's most acclaimed supermodel.'

'Fancy that…' Letty said noncommittally, determined not to react although she had felt the blood draining out of her face as her aunt spoke. Even before the brittle blonde had dropped her bombshell about Leo's mistress, Letty had suspected from her tart defensive tone that Elexis had wanted Leo much more than he had ever wanted her and that her ego had been stung by his walking away from her. The blonde's final words made that reality clear.

As Elexis drifted off, seemingly happy to have stuck the knife in Leo's bride, Letty's attention strayed towards Mariana Santos, a gorgeous brunette with a curvier figure than was usual for a model, her hourglass shape artfully revealed by a turquoise dress with a plunging neckline. Her tummy curdled and she glanced away, annoyed that Leo could be that insensitive. If Elexis knew the identity of his current lover, others had to know as well and it was disrespectful, at the very least, to include such a woman on the guest list. It was not that she felt jealous or possessive of Leo, Letty assured herself as she lifted her chin, a combative glint in her green eyes, it was simply a question of what was right and appropriate.

She looked away from the voluptuous model again, reminding herself that Leo's sex life was none of her business. Even so, the awareness that he had invited his lover to their wedding stung like salt on an open wound. *Get over yourself*, she told herself sternly. The wedding ring on her finger had never been intended as a promise that Leo belonged to her in any way. Their marriage was a fake steadily turning into a farce, she ruminated. So far, she had met Leo's infatuated stepmother, the jealous and spiteful Elexis and now she had Mariana Santos covertly sending the bridegroom a look of burning longing.

Leo had a toxic effect on women, she decided. A little taste of Leo and it seemed women tended to become strongly attached to him and then pine for him. Her nose wrinkled and she thanked her lucky stars that she was not so easily impressed. If that was true, why was she stressing about his obvious compelling attraction in the eyes of *other* women? It shouldn't bother her, should it? She should be able to ignore those other women and not care. Letty swallowed hard, unable to fathom her own reactions and annoyed that the indifference she needed to project towards Leo with regard to his extra-marital interests was nowhere to be found. If she was annoyed, *why* was she annoyed?

That thorny question occupied her brain throughout the reception that followed. It swept her through the wedding speeches and her mother's brief tribute, which brought tears to her daughter's eyes. She strayed into a polite conversation with Leo's father, Panos, and her own grandfather, who it seemed was in a rather glum mood because Leo had recently uncovered some financial irregularities within his company, which Isidore felt he should've discovered for himself.

'Leo's got fantastic financial ability,' Panos Romanos contended with a clear pride in his son's abilities that warmed Letty towards the older man.

'Oh, I'm not denying that,' Isidore responded. 'Our businesses couldn't be in stronger hands than his.'

Leo spanned a lean hand across Letty's stiff spine. 'It's time for us to open the dancing,' he murmured softly in her ear. 'One more hour and then we're out of here.'

Letty twisted her head, eyes wide with surprise. 'Only an hour… Where are we going?'

'Ios…the island,' Leo told her as he urged her on to the dance floor, wondering why she was pulling back from him to ensure a large space separated them.

'But we can't *both* leave the children!' Letty exclaimed.

'They're coming too,' Leo soothed, long brown fingers smoothing down her arms in a curiously caressing motion that sent the oddest little shiver shooting down her taut spinal cord. 'The kids, the nannies, the whole shebang… Happy now?'

'But I didn't do any packing for them and they probably need new clothes *and*—' she began in bemusement.

'That's why I employ staff. It's all taken care of for us,' Leo soothed, lowering his dark head, tawny eyes ablaze with gold below the lights, enhanced by the black lace frame of his lashes. 'And once we arrive I will finally have you all to myself, *yineka mou*.'

Letty stared up at him in confusion, questioning why he would make such a statement and ducking her head to peer around him to see if there was someone nearby for whom he might be putting on an act. Why else would he say such a thing? Coincidentally, Mariana Santos was only a couple of feet away, dancing in the arms of another man, and Letty received a frozen look from the brunette, who had clearly been watching the bridal couple closely. Of course she was, Letty reflected ruefully. Leo was much more Mariana's property than he would ever be his wife's but in public he would pretend otherwise. She marvelled that Mariana had attended the wedding to watch her lover becoming the husband of another woman.

Indeed, so busy was Letty's brain that when Leo kissed her she didn't even see it coming. One minute she was wondering what it was like to be a mistress… and the next? Leo was crushing her parted lips under his with an urgency that shocked her rigid, all that explosive passion of his smouldering and burning through her cool front and smashing it to broken pieces. She swayed, knees turning weak, the sudden pulse of answering heat low in her pelvis a treacherous self-betrayal.

It was just one little kiss and she swiftly tugged free of him and grabbed the back of a convenient chair to steady herself. For a split second she had been shattered by an urgent desire to flatten Leo to the nearest horizontal surface and have her way with him so thoroughly that he would never look at another woman again. And that dangerous thought stayed with her as she recovered from his sensual onslaught. Physically she was fine but mentally she was in another place, she recognised unhappily. He had only kissed her as part of the wedding show. Possibly he had kissed her too because Mariana was nearby, and he intended to make some sort of statement.

But as Letty went upstairs to the room where she was to change, she was much more bothered by her own response to Leo. There was the lust she evidently couldn't suppress and *that* thought she had succumbed to in the same moment…an utterly pathetic and inappropriate desire to have Leo all to herself. In other words, while she was thinking with disdain of all the other women still caught in the trap of craving Leo's blazingly sexual energy, *she* was no better and had absolutely no reason to feel even slightly superior…

CHAPTER SIX

IN THE BIG villa sited on the hill above the bay, Leo grabbed Letty's hand when she would have followed the children and the nannies upstairs. 'No, they've had enough of your attention for one day. Those kids were a nightmare to travel with,' he said with a decided wince.

'*Because*,' Letty replied with emphasis, 'they were overtired and overexcited and the journey totally disrupted their routine.'

'Sometimes schedules have to be disrupted,' Leo countered lazily, tugging her inexorably back to the entrance door and the darkness outside, which had prevented her from seeing much of the island as they flew in on a helicopter. 'This was a special day and you wanted to share it with them. The downside of that decision was their exhaustion.'

Letty nodded, silently conceding that but more curious about where he was trying to take her. 'Where on earth are we going?'

Leo recalled the flight out to Greece and the cross crying, continual demands and screaming from the children and gritted his teeth. Parenting was tougher than he had ever imagined but he was adapting because he hadn't once contemplated leaving his nieces and nephews behind in London. Instead he had come up with a compromise for their honeymoon that would give Letty and him some much-needed space. Not for the first time that day his head spun with a definite sense of wonderment at the commitment he was about to make—one he had never anticipated. It was a huge step for him and he was still marvelling at the aware-ness that such an idea had even occurred to him.

'There's a guest cottage on the beach. We're stay-ing there.'

'But we have to be here with the children,' Letty began afresh.

Leo froze and turned back to her. 'I am delighted that you have already become so fond of the children,' he admitted truthfully. 'But it would be good if you could concentrate...*occasionally*...on my needs.'

Her lashes fluttered in sheer bewilderment. 'But why would I want to do that?' she whispered as he urged her into the beach buggy awaiting them out-side the villa.

'We'll discuss that over dinner,' Leo assured her smoothly as the driver took off down a sloping trail.

Why on earth would he ask her to concentrate on him and his needs? Letty was utterly bewildered. Did he see that as some fundamental rule for an award-winning wife? Was she supposed to be considering *his* comfort 'occasionally' more than the well-being and security of the children? That was very possible, she conceded with a faint sigh of relief that she had finally grasped what he was driving at in his expectations of her. Really, sometimes, Leo was *hopeless* at commu-nication! She supposed it was a reasonable request that she not put the kids first in every case and allow that now and again, much as Leo clearly loved the children and rejoiced in a wealth of nannies, he would appreciate some adult freedom and peace. In any case, she resolved, she could get up early in the morning and join the children for breakfast.

'So, what's this guest cottage all about?' she asked as they climbed out of the buggy and had their luggage offloaded and carried into the substantial natural stone building sited on the edge of the beach.

'My mother liked to paint and it was originally built as an art studio. Katrina renovated it and used it for guests. She had a great need to eradicate anything that reminded her that she was my father's *second* wife,' he stated grimly. 'Strictly speaking, any changes to the properties here were illegal because even as a child the island was mine but, realistically, I was never going to prosecute my father.'

'I suppose you would've liked to inherit it as your mother left it,' Letty gathered quietly, picking up on Leo's innate protectiveness when it came to anything relating to his mother's memory. 'But you knew your father couldn't stand up to Katrina's more forceful character.'

'In a nutshell,' Leo agreed as the door to the softly lit interior was opened and the luggage was piled in and carted upstairs. 'Dad's a wimp when it comes to Katrina.'

In silence Letty raised a brow, able to recognise how much Leo despised his father's weakness when it came to Katrina and belatedly grasping that over the years he had come to regard his dead mother as a complete saint and a wronged woman.

The accommodation might not have been in the

state which Leo would have preferred to inherit but it was contemporary and very stylish and, in Letty's humble opinion, quite beautiful, with floor-deep windows overlooking the sea and the shore. The table at the far end was already set for a candlelit meal. She wondered who was providing the food and then heard noises of activity emanating from what appeared to be a kitchen to the rear. She was relieved not to have to cook because she was tired and she doubted that Leo, raised with attentive staff from birth, even knew how to switch on a kettle. He genuinely had grown up in a different world from hers.

'Have I time to freshen up?' Letty asked, already halfway up the spiral staircase.

'Yes. I could use a shower too,' Leo admitted, following her.

At the top of the staircase, Letty gazed in astonishment at the huge bedroom. Only *one* bedroom? Only *one* bed? Surely not? She slowly turned and watched Leo calmly stripping off his suit jacket and yanking off his tie as if she were invisible. She bent down to open a case and extracted a change of clothing, wondering if they were only to dine at the guest cottage and sleep up at the house, but there was something awfully like a statement about the fresh flowers on display and what looked like herbs or something scattered across the fancy silk cover on the bed. Of course, the staff would assume it was a normal marriage with a normal wedding night, Letty conceded, quelling her unease as Leo got naked right in front of her as if that too was quite normal.

Maybe he assumed that because she was training as a doctor she had few inhibitions about the human body, but Letty was shy, sexually inexperienced, and the sight of Leo's lean, bronzed and very muscular physique naked brought her out in goosebumps of awareness. She hastened into the bathroom, considered locking the door and then abandoned the concept because she wasn't a child or a frightened teenager, was she? He could use the shower—she could *share* the facilities, couldn't she?

In haste she used the shower, scared the door would open but it didn't, and then, in even greater haste, she donned a blue cotton maxi dress that she had bought with her own money to relax in. Leo's credit cards had purchased all the wedding finery as if money were no object and she supposed to him it wasn't. But expressing that little bit of independence had helped her come to terms better with the prospect of a new moneyed lifestyle which she hoped to become used to one small step at a time because spending was still so foreign to her. She had never had money to spend freely, had always had to live on a strict budget. She unwound her hair from its elaborate upswept bridal style and massaged her stiff neck muscles before walking out to the bedroom again.

Leo was out on the balcony beyond the bedroom, still stark naked and nonchalant as he gazed out to sea. Her breath feathered in her throat. He was like… *perfect*—she selected the word inwardly, her cheeks burning. A flawless pinup for an anatomy lesson. No longer need she wonder at the attachment women developed for him. Clothed, he was a very sexy box of tricks. Unclothed, he was undeniably gorgeous, every honed powerful line of him revealed.

'You're very shy…' Leo breathed in apparent surprise when her flushed face met his and she glanced hurriedly away again, terrified her thoughts were showing in her expression. 'I'm sorry... I didn't think—'

He was more sensitive than she had given him credit for, Letty acknowledged, and she smiled. 'No harm done. We're supposed to be married. I'm sure there'll be occasions when we have to share...er...stuff.'

'We *are* married,' Leo reminded her as if she might forget.

'I'll see you downstairs,' Letty breezed with determination, mortified by the reality that she was behaving like a shrinking violet simply because he had undressed. Naturally, he wouldn't have been expecting that, probably having assumed that she had had a man or two in her bed, and she wasn't going to admit that she was a virgin because there was no reason for her to share such an irrelevant fact with him.

Unsurprisingly, Leo was accustomed to experienced women—women who probably stared and mentally oohed and aahed over his magnificent body. Modesty wasn't a skill he had ever needed to learn, and he had, she strongly suspected, few inhibitions in the bedroom. As she sat down at the exquisitely set table, she smiled to herself. She needed to practise being less hidebound and conventional around Leo.

Leo came down again, garbed in jeans and a black shirt and still barefoot, black hair damp from the shower. He had shaved though, the dark stubble that had started to noticeably shadow his strong jawline gone. His lean, darkly arresting features held her gaze and only when she registered that she was staring did she hurriedly look away and address herself to the food now being brought to the table.

'It feels so weird being waited on all the time,' she confided.

'You won't mind it once you return to your studies,' Leo forecast. 'By the way, how is that going?'

'Hopefully, I'll be able to take up my studies again in London next year,' Letty told him cheerfully. 'I didn't have time to get in more than my application before the wedding and there'll be interviews and probably refresher classes and various hurdles to get past before I can start back. I'm lucky my academic record is good.'

There was no luck about it, Leo reflected wryly, wondering why she was so diffident about her achievements. Letty was extremely clever, had been top of her class in just about every subject at Oxford and had won several awards during her time there.

'Let's drink to that,' Leo suggested, nudging her untouched glass with his own. 'Go on, a couple of glasses isn't likely to have a dangerous effect on you.'

Letty coloured to the roots of her hair, knowing that both of them were recalling that encounter in the limousine after her hen party. Leo read her well: he had guessed that she was nervous of alcohol now.

She snatched up her glass and sipped. 'So, you said we had something to discuss… I seem to recall,' she managed to say, relieved that she had stopped squirming and blushing like a teenager over that episode in the car.

'*Ne*…yes,' Leo translated for her as he subsided into Greek and seemed to hesitate as he searched for words, which was sufficiently unlike him to command her full attention and etch a frown between her fine brows. 'It relates to our future as a couple…'

'Yes, I'm sure there must be lots of little things we still have to iron out,' Letty conceded with innate practicality.

'This is not a *little* thing,' Leo contradicted, studying her with dark golden eyes that were pure golden enticement in the candlelight.

'Oh?' Letty prompted, sipping her wine assiduously, irritated that Leo had guessed how she felt about alcohol after the virtual assault she had mounted on him. She pinned her attention to her plate and worked through the delicious first course and a silence that stretched much longer than she had expected.

Finally, Letty looked up again to catch Leo still studying her as though she were a complete mystery to him in some way. 'You were saying?'

Leo breathed in deep and threw back his handsome dark head, his eyes gleaming. 'I don't think I'll ever enter "sacred bond" territory in the manner that you meant,' he murmured smoothly. 'But I have reached the conclusion that it would only be practical for us to at least have a go at making this a *real* marriage.'

Letty literally froze with her glass halfway to her mouth. 'A *real* marriage?' she exclaimed.

'A marriage in which we have sex,' Leo specified with unashamed clarity.

Letty breathed in so deep she was surprised that she didn't spontaneously combust into flames of outrage. 'You have a mistress,' she reminded him tartly.

Leo didn't bat a single eyelash. 'Not currently.'

'That's a lie!' Letty shot back at him. 'Elexis pointed Mariana out to me at the wedding.'

A dark frown formed on Leo's lean strong face. 'That was spiteful,' he breathed with visible annoyance. 'But I'm not lying. I was last with Mariana *before* I met you and I finished with her *after* I met you.'

'Which is…what? All of four short weeks ago?' Letty sniped, unimpressed. 'So, why was she at our wedding?'

'She wasn't invited. She came with a male guest who *was*,' Leo clarified. 'I was irritated when I saw her too.'

Letty recognised the truth when she was hearing it and absolved Leo of inappropriate behaviour because, evidently, Mariana Santos had become old history. Not that that had the slightest cooling effect on her growing anger. That Leo could simply sit there and just proclaim that they should 'have a go' at being married as if it were a casual takeaway meal he could sample at will shocked her to the core.

The main course was brought out and Letty started eating again, although she was barely able to chew and swallow because she was so very angry with him.

'You have nothing to say to my suggestion?' Leo finally pressed in frustration.

'Nothing you'd want to hear,' Letty assured him curtly, pushing her plate away and lifting her glass because she needed a vat of wine, she told herself, to deal with Leo, who was twisty and manipulative and clever and utterly unaccustomed to any form of rejection from a woman.

'Allow me to decide that,' Leo urged.

Letty leapt out of her chair with her glass in one hand, unable to sit still any longer, and she crossed the room to stand by the patio doors. 'We signed a legal agreement in which I agreed to overlook your infidelity,' she reminded him stubbornly. 'Now you want something else from me, something completely different.'

Leo sprang upright. 'I want *you*, so kill me for it!' he urged with sardonic bite, spreading his arms and splaying his expressive hands as part of the gesture.

'You'll want me for all of five minutes!' Letty told him tartly.

'I last longer than five minutes,' Leo assured her, refusing to take that comeback seriously.

And at that provocative sally something Letty had never felt before erupted inside her like a volcano spewing lava. It could only have been described as hissing, spitting rage. She flung what remained of her wine at him. 'You bastard!' she launched at him as the clear liquid splashed his face. 'I trusted you to keep your word but now you're trying to move the goalposts, which is totally unfair to me. And over what? *Sex?*' Letty grimaced in dismissal of that paltry motivation. 'Just because you're between mistresses? What else would suddenly make me so irresistible?'

'It's not like that,' Leo delivered harshly. 'I wanted you the first time I met you and I fought it. Now we're married and it doesn't make sense for me to go out and look for another mistress when the only woman I want right now is *my* wife.'

'Don't you dare call me *your* wife!' Letty fired back at him hotly. 'I married you to be a mother to your sister's children and that was all you asked of me. I'm entitled to receive the agreement I signed up to and the terms I legally approved. You are *not* entitled to demand anything more from me. Is that clear?'

Shocked, Leo scrutinised her, registering that her passion that night in the limo should have forewarned him that she could have a much more tempestuous nature than he had initially appreciated.

'Yes, I can see you're shattered by that news. You know *why*, Leo? Women are too easy for you. Today, in the space of a few short hours, I had Mariana, Katrina and my Aunt Elexis all drooling over you and hating me for marrying you.'

'Is that my fault?' Leo asked with the first hint of anger he had shown. 'Is it my fault that two women I have never been intimate with lust after me? Am I supposed to apologise for that? Clearly, it annoyed you, *but—*'

'I didn't say it annoyed me,' Letty bit out in haste, recognising that she had hit the wall with that comment because it really wasn't fair to blame *him* for being gorgeous and rich and highly desirable to other women. 'What annoys me is that with clear forethought and planning you brought me here to a house with *one* bed and *one* bedroom in expectation of a positive answer!'

'*Theé mou*…there's nothing positive about your attitude,' Leo acknowledged grimly, his lean dark face set in forbidding lines. 'In fact, everything you think about yourself and my interest in you and our marriage is incredibly negative in tone. I didn't mention my intentions *before* the wedding because I had to stay in Greece until shortly before it and it was scarcely a subject I could tackle on the phone.'

'Whatever!' Letty waved an angrily dismissive hand and hauled open the patio doors to walk down onto the sand, desperate for some fresh air and the space to think after that incredibly volatile rush of rage that had so disconcerted her, never mind him.

'It's dark out there!' Leo asserted in warning from behind her.

Letty swung her head back, her honey-blonde mane fluttering in the cool breeze, green eyes gleaming like sea glass polished by the surf. 'I'm not thinking of going for a swim!'

She stomped along the beach, powered by anger, frustration and a whole host of other emotions she could not immediately neatly label and identify. *How dare he?* She grimaced. Leo would always *dare*. Leo didn't respect boundaries and assumed every woman was available should he show interest. But, even if that had been his experience, he shouldn't assume the same thing about *her*!

And then that mortifying incident in the limo returned to haunt her and she groaned out loud because she had given him very willing signals that night, making it obvious that she was attracted to him. Perhaps it wasn't quite so shocking that Leo had expected a positive response from her when she had already given him that much encouragement.

She hitched up her skirt as her heels sank into the sand and, with a muttered curse, bent down to flip off her shoes and walk barefoot, her shoes dangling in one hand.

Slowly, her breathing steadied and her heartbeat stopped thumping madly in her ears. Mariana was no longer his mistress and her departure from the scene had created a vacancy, which Leo hoped to fill with her. It was a practical proposition from a man who clearly saw sex as a need that had to be met. She didn't think that he attached much more importance to sex than that or that he was offering to throw anything more lasting into the mix. Yet the suggestion that they make their marriage the real deal was *still* light years removed from what he had originally proposed. And that made Letty intensely curious to know what it was about her which had brought about that amazing change in attitude.

It was about her—it truly *was* about her. Leo had the hots for her and a choked little giggle erupted in the back of her throat, making her feel remarkably like a teenager again. She raised her brows and continued walking, although her pace had slowed. In the sense that Leo was highly desirable in his own right, his interest made her feel ridiculously flattered but, in another sense, it offended her. If they had sex, and she was honest enough to admit to herself that she was physically willing, where did they go from there? That was the *big* question.

Back at the beach house, Leo tossed back a brandy and paced, wondering where he had gone wrong in his approach because Letty had gone up in flames and that had never happened with a woman before, most definitely not when he was trying to show a woman attention. Was she still so locked into that 'sacred bond' viewpoint that she could not see past it to appreciate that there were other kinds of relationships that functioned perfectly well without twinned souls and romance and all the rest of that nonsense? Leo reasoned impatiently. In a sudden movement, he set down the glass and strode down onto the sand.

Registering that she was cold, for an October night on a Greek island was not that warm with a breeze blowing, Letty had started walking back towards the house. Seeing Leo's tall powerful figure approaching in the moonlight, she sighed and wondered what she was going to say to him.

'I am not an unreasonable woman,' she told him before he reached her. 'If we make this a real marriage, where do we go from there?'

'I don't have a crystal ball,' Leo told her succinctly.

'No, but you do have to think deeply about what you're doing,' Letty countered. 'And I've yet to be convinced that you *do* think that much when it comes to women.'

'*Theé mou...*' Leo ground out.

'You would have to promise to be faithful,' Letty informed him ruefully. 'But you said you couldn't do that.'

'No, I said I didn't want to risk breaking a *promise* of fidelity,' Leo qualified. 'That was what that clause in the prenup meant.'

'That still won't work for me. Either you're mine or you're not mine. There's no halfway house option on offer.'

Surprisingly, Leo felt amusement lick up through his dark mood of dissatisfaction. 'You drive a hard bargain.'

'But you expected that from me,' she guessed.

A wolfish grin slanted Leo's wide sensual mouth and he jerked his chin in acknowledgement. 'If I am with you, I will be with no other woman,' he intoned. 'If I am not content with that, however—'

Shivering, Letty lifted a determined hand to silence him. '*No*, you don't get to qualify it with me. It's either yes or no; you're all in or all out, no escape clauses, no excuses. But that's not all I have to say. Are you viewing this marriage as a temporary aberration or as something that could have a future?'

Leo expelled his breath in audible frustration, his lean dark features taut as he started unbuttoning his shirt. 'I don't know the answer to that.'

'I don't want to enter into a "try before you buy" scenario, Leo. I'm worth more than that,' Letty assured him, throwing her head high, her honey-blonde tresses blowing in the breeze, her clear gaze reflecting the light bouncing off the sea. 'I won't come cheap or easy. I'll make demands. I'll have expectations. I have no idea how a mistress behaves but I would imagine that if a woman is dependent on a man's continuing interest she has to refrain from demands and expectations.'

Leo slid fluidly out of his shirt and draped it round her in a gesture that startled her. 'You're cold,' he said simply.

'I assumed it would be warmer,' she admitted as he closed an arm around her to walk her back towards the beach house. 'But my winter clothes would be too warm.'

'I'll take you shopping,' Leo told her calmly. 'So, *yineka mou*, if I'm now yours, what next have you in store for me?'

Letty chuckled. 'I was rather hoping you'd take the lead there. I haven't had sex before.'

Halfway into the house again, Leo stopped dead and turned to look at her with startled dark golden eyes. 'You mean—?'

'Yes. No experience at all,' she admitted with an uneasy shrug.

Leo was frowning. 'But why?'

'Wasn't interested enough to bother before. Clearly,' Letty murmured with hot cheeks, '*you* float my boat, which is very apt for a shipping tycoon.'

Leo laughed with rich appreciation and swept her towards the stairs. 'I can't wait to get you into that bed,' he admitted frankly. 'Since that night in the car, you've been playing a leading role in all my fantasies.'

Warmth filtered into Letty's chilled body at the concept of figuring in Leo's fantasies. She guessed that it was the unexplored sensual side of her nature which enjoyed that admission of his and then she drew in a stark breath, wondering how he would react when he realised that she was a perfectly ordinary young woman with no box of bedroom tricks with which to amuse a sophisticate. Would he stay faithful then? She swallowed hard on her insecurities, censuring herself for holding such a low opinion of her own powers of attraction. Maybe sex was just sex to Leo and he didn't look for bells and whistles as well, but it was hard to credit that a practised lover couldn't offer much more than she could.

'Leo…' she began anxiously.

'Stop fretting, Letty,' Leo urged with his glimmering smile. 'Don't spoil the moment. I will also be sure to discreetly break the news to your grandfather that you came to me pure as the driven snow. That will set him back on his heels and teach him to respect you more.'

'Leo, for goodness' sake!' Letty broke in, mortified by the idea.

'No, you should be proud rather than apologetic or embarrassed,' her bridegroom told her with conviction as he closed a hand over hers to tug her inexorably up the stairs. 'I haven't been with a virgin since my own first experience. I was sixteen and in the grip of first love. It was a demoralising episode.'

'Why?' Letty asked starkly.

'She was lying—she wasn't a virgin, and within the space of a week she was bedding one of my friends,' Leo confided with a sardonic slant to his lean dark features. 'Following on from my dysfunctional relationship with my stepmother, who was already giving me the come-on, it soured my outlook on women. I promised myself that I'd never fall in love again and I turned my back on the sentimental stuff. It was the most sensible move I ever made.'

Letty put that little fact along with the other stuff she had garnered about Leo's background: the licentious and vindictive stepmother he had endured in his infatuated father's hasty second marriage, the mother he barely remembered, the disillusionment provided by his first love. Grief and hurt and distaste had made him distrustful and pessimistic and his experiences as an adult had only reinforced that outlook. Yet, at the same time, he loved his nephews and nieces enough to surrender his freedom in an attempt to give them a happier and more secure life. There were two sides to Leo, Letty acknowledged, a loving side and a dark cynical side, and she wondered which side would take precedence in their marriage.

A practical sexless marriage about to become a *real* marriage. The shock of realisation that she was about to embark on that challenge shrilled through her taut length and jolted her because she was taking a risk on Leo, and Letty generally avoided risks. And Leo was a *huge* risk, a man only prepared to accept the concept of fidelity at the point of a gun. In a tempest of doubt, Letty turned pale and flicked at one of the dried flowers scattered across the silky bedspread.

'What are these?'

'Rosemary.' Leo shrugged. 'An ancient Greek belief in the power of rosemary to enhance fertility.'

'I thought rosemary was for remembrance,' Letty muttered uncertainly. 'But I suppose I should mention that I'm not on the pill.'

Leo laughed with rich appreciation, dark golden eyes alight with amusement. 'With four little children up in that house on the hill, that's not a risk I will take...unless, of course, you ask me to.'

Letty coloured. 'Er...no, thanks, not just yet.'

'Relax,' Leo purred, enclosing her taut body in the circle of his arms. 'You don't have to worry about stuff like that. I will take care of everything.'

Letty bridled at that assurance, her fierce independent spirit rebelling. 'I take care of myself, Leo,' she said drily.

Leo quirked an ebony brow. 'Not any more. That's my department now.'

'We'll see,' Letty muttered.

'No, we won't,' Leo contradicted, long brown fingers knotting into the breeze-blown tangle of her hair to tug her head back as he crushed her parted lips under his, every ounce of mastery in his erotic repertoire powering that kiss.

CHAPTER SEVEN

HEATED ARGUMENT WAS swirling in Letty's busy brain and then she was pierced by heat of a different kind.

A long shiver snaked through her and she trembled, desire like a living flame flaring low in her belly. She didn't understand her response or the sudden dimming of rational thought and, being Letty, she struggled to comprehend how her physical response could overwhelm her mental reactions. And in that moment of disconcerted stasis Leo tangled his tongue with hers, skated it over the roof of her mouth and her legs literally went weak. Ultimately that didn't matter because he was already leaning her up against him for support while tugging down the straps on her maxi dress and letting it fall to the floor.

Eyes fluttering in dismay, Letty found herself lying back on the bed with no clear awareness of how she had arrived there. She gazed up at Leo worriedly, painfully sober, painfully aware of the size of her bare breasts, which had always been larger and more noticeable than she was comfortable with, but then bosomy women ran in the family genes and she hadn't got a choice in the matter.

'*Theé mou...*' Leo groaned with unashamed appreciation. 'You have gorgeous breasts.'

Taken aback, Letty peered down at her attributes in bewilderment as Leo curved what could only be described as reverent hands to the bountiful swell of her breasts, shaping and moulding them, fingers grazing the stiffened peaks, lingering to rub the sensitive tips and provoke a breathy gasp from her lips as an arrow of heat ran down to her pelvis. Leo liked her body, Leo accepted her as she was, and a whole slice of her anxiety fell away in that moment. He closed his mouth to a tender pink nipple and she jerked in surprise, unprepared for the pulsing ache stirring at the heart of her body.

A sensual daze cocooned her as a tightening sensation banded her womb, her hips pushing up for relief as he teased a swollen bud with the edge of his teeth and moved hungrily to the other. Answering heat sizzled through her quivering body before the slowly heightening delight just seemed to explode deep down inside her, sending streamers of multi-coloured fire darting through every nerve-ending she possessed and dragging a cry from deep in her throat. Stray convulsions of pleasure continued to tug at her as she flung her head back in reaction, her honey-blonde mass of hair spreading across the pillows in a silken tangle.

'You're very sensitive there, *meli mou*,' Leo murmured with satisfaction, long fingers gently brushing an almost painfully tender pink nipple. 'I love that.'

Letty lifted a hand to frame one high cheekbone, utterly mesmerised by the smouldering blaze of his dark golden eyes. Her other hand curved to a bare bronzed shoulder with a new sense of intimacy that pleased her almost as much as it unnerved her. She liked the feel of his hot smooth skin and that was fine, perfectly acceptable as long as she accepted that that physical connection was as much as she could allow herself to feel for him.

'What are you thinking about?' Leo demanded with a disconcerted frown.

'Nothing, nothing at all,' Letty fibbed, lashes veiling her eyes as she drew herself up to put her lips against his again and he took the bait with alacrity, kissing her breathless while her restive hands roved over the smooth taut muscles of his spine to inch down into the waistband of his jeans to tug him closer still.

'There's so much more for us to discover,' Leo murmured huskily, darting a trail of kisses down the slope that ran from her ear to her shoulder, singling out sensitive spots that even she had not known she possessed and reawakening the hunger he had briefly sated.

Somewhere during that moment, her last garment disappeared but she was much more preoccupied by the line of kisses Leo was tracing down over her midriff to the honeyed, throbbing core of her. She closed her eyes tight, surrendering control for the first time ever, knowing that the more aroused she was, the easier her introduction to sex would be. Before very long, she was no longer capable of such practical reflections and her body was writhing without her at the controls.

Excitement began to build in waves that climbed higher and higher. He slid a finger into her and toyed with the slick damp flesh between her slender thighs. Desire engulfed her in a sharp flood of impatience and frustration. She couldn't stay still—she couldn't stay still long enough to catch her breath and her heart was racing, perspiration breaking out on her skin as the heat mushroomed up from her pelvis and made her fingernails claw into his luxuriant hair.

'Just do it!' she told him fiercely. 'I'm not expecting rainbows and unicorns!'

'Which is why we're doing it my way,' Leo countered with ferocious amusement.

With difficulty, Letty overcame a mortifying sense of being out of her depth and hating that almost as much as she loved what he was doing to her. Being in bed with Leo was one of the biggest learning experiences of her life, teaching her how much she had underestimated the power of desire to seduce. In a daze and still on the crest of an almost unbearable high of physical responsiveness, she watched Leo reach for protection and roll back to thrust his jeans out of his path with something less than the cool and control she had expected from him.

And then he came back to her with a hungry demanding urgency that taught her that, regardless of his patience, he was every bit as fiercely aroused as she was. He rearranged her with deft hands, scored an expert fingertip over the throbbing bud and triggered a breath-stealing climax that blew her away seconds before he angled his lean hips and filled her in one smooth motion. The sharp stab of pain was lost in a welter of other sensations that consumed her and within seconds he was tilting her up to drive in deeper with restrained thrusts.

He groaned something in Greek but Letty was way beyond asking him to translate, far too concentrated as she was on the eddying pulse of pleasure picking up pace with his every fluid movement. She arched up with a long gasping sigh to greet the wildly sensual and satisfying slam of his body into hers and the all-consuming excitement fired her afresh. He shifted to sink into her receptive core from another angle and grind down on her and her body ignited like oil thrown on a bonfire, tightening and burning and flying into renewed release.

Afterwards she wasn't quite sure what planet she was on, even if she was actually present with her own body because she felt weirdly insubstantial and detached from the world. She was drained, exhausted but somehow happy in a way she had never known before. For the first time ever she didn't feel alone, and the arms she had linked round Leo stayed in place until he pulled away, rolling off the bed to stride into the bathroom. Safe sex, she reminded herself. Of course the practicalities would disrupt the aftermath.

'Did you catch a distant glimpse of even one tiny rainbow?' Leo murmured huskily as he strode back to the bed.

'The whole sky was full of them,' Letty whispered, suddenly feeling self-conscious, which struck her as ridiculous after the intimacy they had shared. She had known Leo for only a month and already he had turned her inside out and upside down, she conceded worriedly.

Leo came down on the bed beside her again and it occurred to her that everything that had transpired between them had been entirely one-sided. Her face burned with guilt and embarrassment because she had been selfish. Sex was supposed to be a two-way activity and she had barely participated.

An unholy grin slashed his wide sensual mouth as he looked down at her. 'I could swear I saw a unicorn,' he teased.

And Letty shook free of her insecurities and laughed,

responding to the charisma Leo emitted at every turn. Certainly, he knew how to dispel an awkward moment.

'I'd love a rerun,' Leo confided. 'But I know that right now that wouldn't be very comfortable for you.'

Hot colour washed Letty's cheeks and she turned her face into the pillow and curled up. 'I'm exhausted,' she agreed ruefully because she was. Not only had it been a very long day full of stresses and strains but also her relationship with Leo had shifted into dramatically new territory and she wasn't yet sure how she felt about that.

'Sleep,' Leo urged lazily.

Letty would have enjoyed a bath to relax in but that would've entailed getting out of bed naked and crossing the room in front of Leo and she wasn't quite ready for that amount of exposure. He had given her a great deal of pleasure and presumably had taken pleasure in her. Or was it merely a matter of gaining sexual release for Leo? It was better not to dress harsh facts up, she told herself; it would be wiser to remain realistic.

But the knowledge that that was the sensible way to behave didn't prevent Letty from wishing that he would close an arm around her and show her some affection and discovering that need, that craving, inside her chilled her blood. There was no point seeking more from a male who had spelt out the reality that he didn't want or need more, that indeed a bloodless convenient marriage that included sex was the current summit of his ambitions.

At the same time, she ruminated, that prenup agreement she had signed would have to be updated and changed to reflect the major alteration that had taken place in their relationship. Letty looked forward to that.

Even when she had believed that she and Leo would never have a normal marriage, it had gone against the grain to sign any document that sanctioned his infidelity. On that soothing thought of what she viewed as an innate wrong being righted, she went to sleep.

When the phone beside the bed rang in the early hours, Letty, inured to wake-up calls and early rising, answered it immediately before it could disturb Leo. It was one of the nannies. Popi had had a bad dream and was inconsolable. Letty crept out of bed and rustled in her suitcase for sensible clothes before allowing herself a last glance at Leo as he slept in a lazy sprawl that had left her sleeping on the far edge of the bed. She smiled as she hurriedly brushed her hair. Even asleep Leo looked gorgeous, a rumpled sheet barely covering his bronzed and muscular length, his black hair and his stubbled jawline very dark against the pale bedding. She brushed her teeth, regretted that she dared not waste time taking a shower and padded out of the beach house to be greeted by Darius, who looked equally tired at the wheel of the beach buggy that would take her up to the villa.

Popi had got herself really worked up and it took time to calm her, and her sobs had wakened Sybella, who curled up at the foot of the bed once Letty arrived and quietly went back to sleep. Letty rocked Popi until she had recovered enough to make herself understood and then it all came flooding out: the argument she had had with her mother the night of the accident, her fear that her bad behaviour could have somehow caused the tragedy. Letty soothed her with the truth that nothing could've changed events that fatal night and the assurance that her loving mother would've understood her daughter's disappointment at not being allowed to accompany her parents to the hospital to collect her baby brother and bring him home for the first time.

Leo woke at dawn and sat up, surprised to find himself in an empty bed and then furious, stalking into the shower to cool off before pulling on jeans and a shirt. Letty would be with the children, he knew that, but he also knew that they needed to spend alone time as a couple and if she couldn't even go a few hours without checking in with the kids, how were they going to get to know each other? Righteously annoyed, Leo left the beach house and found Darius seated bleary-eyed with lack of sleep on a chair on the veranda.

'Popi had a nightmare,' Darius told him. 'The nanny phoned before I could advise her not to.'

'Go to bed, Darius. You don't need to be on call twenty-four-seven here on the island,' Leo responded ruefully.

'I stayed up to try and prevent you from shooting yourself in the foot,' his oldest friend admitted ruefully.

'And how am I going to do that?'

'You have to share her with the kids and you're accustomed to women who make *you* the centre of their world,' Darius remarked warily.

'There speaks the father,' Leo quipped, for Darius had three children.

Darius stood up and grimaced. 'Children change the dynamics of things,' he said wryly.

Leo knew all about how the arrival of children changed life, but it still bothered him that Darius had stayed out of bed to intercept him before he confronted Letty for sneaking off before their wedding night was even over. Did he seem that intolerant? Was he, in fact, spoiled by too many women who had unquestioningly put him first? Was he suffering from wounded pride? After all, why was he concerned in any way? Everything had gone according to plan and the sex, the marital sex, had been superlative. Letty was also the one and only woman who had ever been his alone and he liked that; indeed he was surprised by how much he had revelled in being the first.

As Leo appeared at the door of his nieces' bedroom, Popi held a finger to her lips, urging his silence. Letty was fast asleep on the little girl's bed with Sybella tucked in at her back. Leo smiled and crossed the room to lift his bride gently off the bed and carry her down the corridor to his bedroom, where he settled her down on the big bed and, as an afterthought, tugged up a throw to toss over her.

Letty stirred, opening drowsy green eyes to take in his vibrant presence.

'Go back to sleep. We're heading out shopping later and you'll need your energy.'

Her smooth brow furrowed. 'Shopping?'

'You need clothes,' Leo reminded her.

'I should tell you about Popi's nightmare first.'

'Later...' Leo stressed. 'She's quite happy now.'

Letty subsided back against the pillows.

'I also thought we could consider consulting the island doctor. You may deem it safer to take the contraceptive pill,' Leo framed with caution.

'Yes...that would be a good idea,' Letty conceded, thinking that the last thing they needed was an unplanned pregnancy but that, in time, she would probably want to have her own baby. A family of five and a career and Leo into the bargain? She almost rolled her eyes at that enormous challenge. Other women coped though and so would she and she could hardly complain when she would have all the help she needed on the home front.

By that afternoon, they were walking into a designer atelier in Athens, where Leo was received like returning royalty. That started her thinking that Leo was disturbingly knowledgeable about where to buy expensive female clothing. The thought made her uncomfortable because it reminded her of her many predecessors. She swallowed hard, conceding that, for a womaniser, such familiarity went with the territory.

She was disconcerted to recognise her aunt, Elexis Livas, in conversation with a fawning assistant, a tall, voluptuous brunette by her side. The brunette instantly gave Leo her attention, throwing him a lingering look and a flirtatious smile before breaking away from Elexis to say, 'I wasn't expecting to see you here today, Leo. Elexis has been telling me all about the wedding.'

'Letty…' Leo murmured smoothly. 'Dido Bakas… How's the theatre run going?'

'Brilliantly!' Dido exclaimed, resting a hand on Leo's sleeve with the familiarity of a lover. 'You should try to make the show before it closes. I'd love to see you in the audience.'

Letty felt invisible. The other woman had ignored her extended hand and continued to focus solely on Leo.

'Sadly, I'm a little too busy right now,' Leo parried as Elexis joined them.

'I can't believe you're out and about the day after the wedding,' Elexis commented, shooting Letty an amused look as if it were a mortification for a bride-groom to be seen in public so soon after the wedding.

'Letty doesn't enjoy shopping, so I'm here to do it for her,' Leo said lightly. 'Excuse me. We have a private viewing organised and we're running a little late.'

'Are you sure you can't make it to my engagement party on Saturday?' Elexis pressed, big brown eyes pinned to Leo as though he hung the moon.

'Unfortunately, we have a prior engagement,' Leo countered. 'My new nightclub is opening up in Athens on Saturday.'

Elexis looked pained. 'But I thought that was next week.'

'I moved it forward. Saturday is Letty's birthday… It seemed fitting to change the date,' Leo suggested lazily, spreading his hand across Letty's taut spine and guiding her towards the woman waiting to welcome them.

'How did you know it was my birthday?' Letty whispered.

'Marriage licence,' Leo told her as they were ushered into a large showroom, shown to seats and offered champagne.

'And you moved the opening date forward?' Letty questioned in disbelief. 'Because of *my* birthday?'

'You're my wife. It seemed appropriate, even if it did cast the organisers into a loop.'

'And we're attending this event together?' Letty prompted.

'Even I would not leave you alone to celebrate your birthday,' Leo chided as models began to stroll out of the changing rooms behind the small catwalk and strut their stuff. It was an entertaining show, but Letty was intimidated by the height and slenderness of the models and could not picture her more ordinary self wearing such elegant, exclusive garments.

Leo, however, had no such inhibitions. He signalled the designer and indicated the outfits he preferred, seemingly impervious to the reality that she was very different in shape from the models and would not look the same.

An assistant escorted her into a changing room to be measured and within a very short space of time she was trying on clothes and the tailor was taking note of the adjustments to be made. A rack of lingerie was brought to her to try on next.

Her phone buzzed while she was striving not to think about Dido, who was clearly an ex of Leo's. It was a text from Leo.

Come out and model the lingerie for me.

Letty was aghast at that suggestion, and the thought of displaying herself that way for Leo made her grow uncomfortably hot. Wide-eyed and flushed, she studied her reflection in the mirror. She was wearing a very pretty bra and briefs combination in pale blue. The bra fitted much better than the bras she usually wore. In fact, it seemed that she had been wearing the wrong size for years.

What's made you so shy?

And Letty went pink. It was as if the wretched man was inside her head, rooting about and forcing her insecurities into the light of day.

In her head was an image of Elexis, pencil-thin in tangerine, and Dido, curvy but still skinny in all the right places with long legs. Letty was different, shorter and rounder, but she was *still* the woman Leo wanted, the woman he had made passionate love to the night before.

Only love had had nothing to do with it, she reminded herself ruefully. Even so, bodies came in all shapes and sizes and she did not like to acknowledge that she had a poor body image or low self-esteem. It was *just*… Her brow furrowed until she understood herself better. It occurred to her, for the very first time, that she *was* actually quite shy but that the need to focus on other people throughout her life had blinded her to that truth. And the women around Leo, the women he had actually been with, seemed so ridiculously beautiful that she was intimidated and shrank from the comparisons.

Enough was enough, Letty decided on the back of that lowering thought, stepping out of the changing room with a sway to her hips and an angle to her chin. And Leo, sprawled in his chair looking bored and clearly not expecting her, sat up with a jerk, stunned by her response to his challenge. And Letty liked that reaction; she liked it very much. She strolled across to the table and lifted her champagne to sip it, gloriously aware that Leo could not take his spectacular dark golden eyes from her.

'So, basic is what turns you on,' Letty murmured with a rueful sigh.

'Pretty much,' Leo admitted, his attention welded to that wondrous hourglass shape of hers and the swell of her breasts.

'At least that's fairly normal,' Letty conceded, empowered by the reality that Leo, basic or otherwise, was visibly aroused. 'At one stage early on I did wonder if you were insisting on keeping a mistress because you were into some sort of kink—'

Leo almost choked on his champagne and hurriedly set down the glass. *'Kink?'* he stressed, his gorgeous eyes bright with disbelief.

'It was a fair enough assumption when I didn't know you,' Letty parried, cool as a cucumber now. 'Want to see anything else?'

'Surprise me again… You keep *on* doing that,' Leo breathed, studying her with intense dark golden eyes. 'I didn't think you'd have the nerve to come out.'

Letty sashayed back to the changing room wearing a grin she wouldn't have shown him for a million pounds. She emerged again in a black set ornamented with shocking pink lace and Leo lounged back in his chair to enjoy the show.

'You do realise that I'm likely to jump you in the limo after this?' he murmured thickly.

'Promises…promises,' Letty countered with a roll of her green sea glass eyes and with more daring than she had known she possessed.

'I can't wait that long,' Leo breathed, striding into the changing room in her wake and catching her into his arms before she could guess his intention.

'You can't…*here*!' Letty gasped, thoroughly disconcerted as he backed her up against the wall, pinning her hands to either side of her and caging her in with his lean powerful body. Yet looking up into the smouldering heat of his eyes, she found his dominance outlandishly sexy.

'Nobody will disturb us,' Leo murmured huskily. 'I only need a little taste of you.'

His mouth crashed down on hers and she strained helplessly against him, a flood of hunger released instantly. He hitched one of her legs up and ground against her and her awareness of his arousal mounted a thousandfold and sent fireworks shooting through her pelvis. His tongue tangled with hers and a low moan escaped her, an ache forming between her taut thighs. He released her hands and glided his fingertips lightly down her ribcage, making her shiver convulsively. Her heart was racing so fast she could hardly catch her breath, and then he touched her where she most needed to be touched and she thought she would spontaneously combust from the surge of tingling tormenting sensation at her core.

Her eyes flicked open on the mirror behind Leo and a belated awareness of where they were engulfed her. She pushed her palms against his chest and looked up at him, hot and flushed and damningly conscious of how much she wanted him.

'Not here,' she muttered tautly.

His body screaming for release, Leo snatched in a ragged breath. He should never have left the island, he recognised, because he couldn't keep his hands off her. That hadn't happened to him with a woman in more years than he could count, and he didn't want it to happen with her. Control was important to Leo. Anything excessive in any aspect of his life set up warning markers he heeded. His father loved his stepmother obsessively and it had meant that the older man made some very bad decisions. Not that Leo was afraid that he could be falling in love—no, far from it. He almost smiled at the idea, knowing himself to be too battle-hardened by far to be prone to that weakness. On the other hand, obsessive lust was dangerous as well.

'We'll get back to Ios,' Leo agreed. 'I'll have the rest of your new wardrobe sent out to the island for you to choose from there.'

Letty seemed transfixed by the idea and her eyes widened. 'I'll get dressed.'

'Yes, that would be sensible,' Leo murmured as if he had never asked her to model the lingerie for him or, indeed, had followed her into the changing room.

Letty was restive in the limo that returned them to the airport because Leo had withdrawn from her. Because she had said no? She didn't think so. She suspected Leo had also succumbed to a moment of temptation and taking account of their surroundings had reined back his desire for her. But she knew he had an apartment in Athens and he didn't suggest heading there and he didn't approach her in the limo either.

Finally, shortly before they reached the airport, she asked him a question that had been playing heavily on her mind. 'I've been wondering...' she began tautly. 'When will you be changing the terms in the prenuptial contract I signed?'

Dark brows pleating, Leo frowned at her in apparent astonishment. 'Why would I do that?'

'Because everything between us has changed,' Letty pointed out simply. 'This is not the detached marriage we originally agreed, and I do not accept your right to be unfaithful now.'

That assurance fell into a bottomless pit of silence.

Leo's dark gaze was hooded and cool. His jawline clenched hard. 'We'll discuss it later, although I should warn you that we have different viewpoints.'

Letty swallowed hard, not liking the sound of that for she couldn't imagine what he could think they *could* have to discuss in the circumstances. He had radically changed the terms of their marriage and she had rights too…*didn't she?*

CHAPTER EIGHT

LETTY REFUSED TO be intimidated by Leo's forbidding coolness on the flight back to the island and she was surrounded by the children when they walked into the big house. Popi, as lively as though that nightmare had never happened, wanted to know where they had been, what they had done, what they had bought. Cosmo had a car to show her. Sybella was lugging around a doll almost as big as she was and Theon just held out his arms to her, always eager for a cuddle.

'We're dining at the beach house,' Leo decreed, unable to hang onto his reserve with Sybella trying to climb up him as if he were a tree.

'Yes,' Letty agreed. 'Later. I'll see the children to bed first...if that's all right with you?'

Leo studied her, a muscle pulling at the edge of his taut jaw. His spectacular bone structure was visible beneath his bronzed skin, his dark golden eyes bright with a glint of impatience. And anger? Well, if he was angry, too bad, Letty reasoned. The prenup stuff had to be dealt with, whether he liked it or not. He jerked his chin in acknowledgement of her plans and swung round, bending to let Sybella slide down from his arms. 'I'll catch up with some work.'

* * *

Why did she want to mess around with the prenup? he was asking himself grimly. It was there as a safeguard, nothing more. Could she already be contemplating divorcing him? Why the urgency? Had he made a crucial mistake choosing Letty as a wife? Why should she hang around, playing mother to four kids who weren't her own, when she could be living the life of a millionaire, free and clear? A dark brooding expression set his lean strong features hard. Why had he been so sure that she was different from other women? Money, after all, was the most persuasive power on the planet for many, many people. It made them turn their back on moral scruples. Yet the children were already attached to Letty, and Popi was finally behaving more like a little girl without the worries of the world weighing down her tiny shoulders.

Nothing was going quite as Leo had planned and he hated that. For a start, he was aware that he had underestimated the importance of the woman he had married and the value of the role she would play in his life. His sex drive had got in the way of pragmatism and possibly put everything else at risk, which was crazy, he acknowledged broodingly. Letty had warned him that she would make demands and have expectations and he hadn't really listened. His sole focus had been on getting her into bed and, even worse, it *still* was. He hadn't counted on wanting Letty as much as he did. Somewhere in the back of his mind he had wondered if a couple of weeks of her would sate him and if he would then eventually return to his former way of life…

Letty resolved to encourage Leo to get more involved with the children's bedtime routine but acknowledged that perhaps today wasn't the right day to make that suggestion. Turning a sophisticated tycoon into a get-down-and-dirty father would be a project and a half, she reflected, but his nieces and nephews did need more than the occasional hug from him.

The children all tucked up, Letty sped down to the beach house with Darius at the wheel of the buggy. He told her about his wife and children who lived on Ios, admitting that his wife refused to move because her family was there, and he travelled a great deal with Leo.

Arriving at the beach house, Letty hurtled upstairs for the shower she was desperate to enjoy. Her suitcases had been unpacked and she rifled through the slender collection of clothes hung for her, recognising that she had seriously misjudged the number of outfits she would need. Of course, that wasn't likely to be a problem once she picked out new clothes. Selecting a flouncy skirt and cotton sweater, she went for a shower and broke out her even smaller collection of cosmetics. A lick of mascara, a touch of blusher and clear lip gloss and she was done. She scrutinised her reflection as she blow-dried her hair.

There was no point in kidding herself that she could compete in the looks department with women like Dido and Mariana. They were dark, she was fair. They were tall, she was short. They were well-groomed and so-phisticated, she was more the girl next door, put together in a hurry and on a wing and a prayer. Would *he* even notice if she put on nail varnish? It would get chipped when she was messing about with the kids. What on earth was that man doing to her priorities? Why she was looking so critically at herself? Why was she only seeing flaws? Well, how was she to help doing so? Right now, she seemed to be continually meeting women like Elexis or Katrina panting for Leo's interest, or exes like Dido and Mariana, more than ready for a sexual rerun with him!

And possibly she had always lacked confidence in herself, she acknowledged for the first time, hiding behind the needs of her family and putting them first. In a sense that attitude and intensive study had provided a shield between her and the world, but that shield was gone now that she was with Leo.

Leo awaited her downstairs, a balloon glass of brandy between his fingers. Just seeing him stopped her dead in her tracks. His luxuriant black hair was still damp and, like her, he had changed, the exquisitely cut designer suit he had worn earlier now replaced by narrow black pants and a white linen shirt left open at the neck.

'A drink?' he enquired.

'Something soft if you have it.' Letty knew that she needed to keep her head clear for the conversation they had to have.

'We don't need drama twenty-four hours into our marriage,' Leo murmured with measured cool. 'You're not giving us a fair crack of the whip.'

Letty paled and stiffened, annoyed by his attitude. 'This is not drama.'

Leo shifted a shoulder in a fluid shrug of brazen disagreement, lean muscles flexing beneath his shirt, and she dragged her attention away from him again, embarrassed by her need to savour him like a starstruck teenager. There would never be another Leo in her life. That went without saying. But she also knew that if their relationship was to have any chance of survival, she had to fight for that chance and ensure that he understood that she was serious.

'In the prenup there was a clause relating to your freedom to sleep with whomever you chose and that not being grounds for divorce,' she reminded him doggedly.

His shrewd gaze widened a little and lingered. 'That was the deal.'

'*Was* being the operative word,' Letty stressed. 'That *was* the deal until *you* changed it last night, when I understood that you are now prepared to commit to this marriage. If that is the case, why do you *still* need that clause?'

'Commitment is a rather strong word,' Leo countered, sipping his brandy. 'In fact, it gives me chills. I've never been committed to anybody but my family.'

'I'm supposed to be your family now,' Letty pointed out stiffly as he passed her a drink.

'Committing to a woman is a tall order. I said I was willing to *try* being married.'

'And I said I wouldn't be part of a "try before you buy" experiment!' Letty riposted in sudden anger. 'This isn't a fluid situation, Leo. You can't keep on changing the terms. You don't want to commit? You don't want to promise fidelity?'

'No. I don't want to hear either of those words,' Leo admitted harshly, thinking of his father's devotion to Katrina and her constant betrayal of his trust, not to mention the many other infidelities he had witnessed in both sexes over the years. 'I will promise not to lie to you. I will promise never to go behind your back. But the best I can do on the fidelity front is to promise that I will always be honest. As I said once before, I can't foretell the future.'

Letty felt as if she had been crushed against a brick wall and suddenly she was reeling with a sense of betrayal. Had she misunderstood him the night before? Surely she had been plain about what *she* wanted and needed? Her oval face tightened, her eyes veiling. 'You know what? That's fine, Leo…' she said limply, turning with relief as the first course of their meal arrived and using the hiatus to take a seat at the beautifully set table.

Leo's tension evaporated. He had been expecting all sorts of things from her other than what he had received. She was still hung up on the fidelity stuff, still striving to idealise their marriage into some perfect picture, but she wasn't thinking of divorce. He refused to label the sensation strongly reminiscent of relief travelling through him. Obviously, he was grateful that she had staying power for the children's sake. But she was still wilfully misunderstanding him, he reasoned in exasperation. It wasn't as though he had any plans to cheat on Letty; he simply preferred complete honesty because he was a cynic about the promises of fidelity that people blithely made and then broke.

Letty shook out her napkin with a flourish, slight colour slowly returning to mantle her cheeks. 'As I said, that's fine. You do what you need to do. But you have to accept that I have certain requirements as well. If you're not prepared to have that clause eliminated from the prenup, then you're clearly not prepared to make a concrete commitment to our marriage. Sorry, did I use that nasty word again?' she said as his arrogant head came up, dark eyes ablaze with gold challenge.

'Letty…' Leo began.

Letty faked a greater interest than she truly felt in her tiny portion of red pepper, feta and olive frittata. In fact, hungry as she was, she was feeling nauseous about the situation she was in and crushingly, horribly *hurt*. As if Leo's refusal to commit was a personal rejection.

'You're making far too much of that clause.'

'I saw it being deleted from the agreement as a pledge, as proof that you were serious in your intentions.'

'I *am* serious in my intentions!' Leo snapped back at her in frustration. 'I said I would *try*.'

Letty leant back in her chair, the delicious bite of pie turning to ashes in her dry mouth. 'And that's not enough for me. We're at a crossroads here. I suggest that we agree to differ, rather than argue a non-negotiable point and—'

Leo thrust away his plate untouched, his dark golden eyes mirroring his turbulent emotions. Letty was putting him through the mill and he hadn't expected that, but this time around he didn't mistake his sense of reprieve for anything other than what it was. 'That would be sensible,' he conceded.

Letty sighed. 'You didn't let me finish, Leo. For us both to be happy in this relationship, we have to compromise. But, since I can't share a bed with a man I can't trust, you will have to embrace your sexual freedom…and we'll never discuss this thorny and distasteful subject again.'

Leo was shattered. He certainly hadn't seen *that* offer coming. He breathed in deep and slow. 'That's not a reasonable compromise, Letty.'

'I can't be reasonable about everything,' Letty said quietly. 'We're compromising. You're getting what you want.'

'*How?* I want *you!*' Leo slung back at her wrathfully, the temper he controlled rigidly breaking free.

'Not as much as you want a get-out clause for when you get bored with me,' Letty qualified without a shade of expression. 'That's how it is. I'm not going to quarrel with you about it.'

'No!' Leo rasped, expelling his breath and thrusting his hands down to rise from his seat, a deep sense of injustice powering him. 'You're only kicking me out of the marital bed for a sin I haven't committed yet!'

'*Yet.*' Letty stressed his use of that word. 'You see, in your mind you're still a free man, *not* a married man. Even worse, you view yourself as a man who cannot be faithful. I would have to be a very stupid woman not to steer clear of that accident waiting to happen… and I'm not stupid, Leo.'

Tied into knots by her words and his own and infuriated by her tranquil attitude when he was ready to punch holes in walls, Leo scrutinised his wife with outraged, dark as jet eyes, faint colour scoring his hard cheekbones. 'I'll have your stuff moved back up to the main house immediately.'

'There's no rush,' Letty told him uneasily.

Leo ate with appetite, even offered occasional conversation. To give him his due, he didn't brood or give her the silent treatment. Letty, however, was under no illusion that what still powered him was anger: he was determined to keep his freedom and she wanted to take it away. There was no possible conciliation between such far-removed objectives. Maybe he needed time and space to consider those facts before he would be willing to acknowledge the good sense of leaving sex out of their marriage. That was what he had first wanted and what she had been happy to accept, but then he had changed his mind and decided he wanted her...and fatally, foolishly, she had decided to give him a chance.

Why? She wanted to box her own ears for her stupidity. She had taken a risk on him, but he had quickly brought her crashing down to earth again.

Her luggage was discreetly carted out while they finished their meal with coffee. It was all very civilised but Letty still felt as though she were the one being kicked out and when Darius drove her back up to the main house his diplomatic silence warned her that, like the rest of the staff, he also knew that the brief honeymoon was over and Letty was mortified by Leo's intransigence and his disinterest in what other people might think. Evidently the pretence that theirs was a normal marriage was already over.

Tears leaked out of the corners of Letty's eyes and stung her quivering cheeks that night as she lay in her new bed. She wouldn't let herself sob or grieve for what had proved to be an empty illusion. She was hurt and she acknowledged that while also acknowledging that she had already become far too attached to Leo in spite of his ferocious stubbornness. She was doing the sensible thing in protecting herself, she told herself.

Leo couldn't sleep. He paced the bedroom floor, trying to pin down the exact moment when everything had gone pear-shaped. It was the first time in his life that that had happened to him with a woman. He was accustomed to calling all the shots, to having exactly what he wanted but Letty didn't work that way. She wanted pledges, sacred bonds, all the rest of that nonsense, he fumed in measured annoyance as he fought a growing sense of injustice.

He couldn't imagine being faithful all his life to one woman. But his overriding belief remained that he did not want to *hurt* Letty or any other woman! As he suspected his mother must often have been hurt by his father's infidelities. Leo had never in his life cheated on any woman, choosing to be honest when he knew he wanted to move on, had never had a desire to have more than one woman at a time in his life.

None of his ancestors, his grandfather or his father, had pledged fidelity. Even so, as far as he knew, his father had always been slavishly faithful to his step-mother, Katrina. But that was only because his father, weak and pathetic man that he was, worshipped the ground that Katrina walked on. And look where that had got the older man: a wife who was well known for her extra-marital affairs! No, he certainly wasn't ready to follow that unpleasant and humiliating example as a blueprint for his future, he assured himself squarely, while stamping firmly down on the knowledge at the back of his mind that Letty wasn't that sort of woman.

Letty had given him one fantastic night and he would have to be content with that. He studied the bed that they had shared and gritted his teeth. He wanted her, he wanted her there now, *ached* just at the thought of reliving that pleasure. But he would get over that, the sneaky type of sexual infatuation she had some-how plunged him into. Because he had been her first? Was that the secret of her intense attraction for him? He didn't know; he only knew he felt angry, frustrated and frazzled and most unlike himself and he *hated* it— absolutely bloody hated it!

* * *

The following morning, all the clothes and accessories arrived for Letty to try on and consider and she was trying to decide between two black cocktail dresses when Leo entered the room with a small warning knock that made her spin round in dismay, the zip she had been struggling with still open and exposing her bare back.

'I'll call your maid.'

Letty laughed. 'No, now you're here…you can make yourself useful. Are you still taking me to that club opening on Saturday?'

Leo raised an ebony brow, clearly surprised that she had assumed that he might have changed his mind on that score. 'Is it still your birthday on Saturday? Then yes, but don't pick a black dress. You need something *more*…' He rifled through the rack of clothes and dragged out a scarlet dress that she wouldn't have considered in a thousand years for her wardrobe. It was stretchy, glittery, low-necked and low-backed, in short everything she avoided.

'Er…no…' She didn't want to hurt his feelings when he was trying to help. 'That's a little daring for me. I mean, look at that neckline.'

'I'm a man—of course I'm looking at the neckline,' Leo reasoned. 'You've got a terrific figure. Wear colours and show it off.'

Letty flushed. 'I'll try it on and see,' she conceded, still doubtful but knowing that that accolade from him would make her more than consider wearing it. Was she a people-pleaser? Or a Leo-pleaser? She only knew that she craved his admiration, which was childish and rather unfair to him when she had refused to sleep with him again.

Leo lifted the house phone and spoke in Greek. 'I've called your maid. Use the staff. That's what they're here for,' he urged.

Letty grimaced. 'It'll take a while for me to get used to having staff around but I'll work on it… OK?'

'OK.' Leo studied her with a totally unreadable expression but his dark golden eyes were alight and she felt that scrutiny make her nipples peak inside her bra and force her to press her thighs together on the ache that stirred in her pelvis.

Of course she was still attracted to him and *that* was going to happen, she reminded herself, but eventually she would get a handle on such responses, wouldn't she? And, under all the surface sophistication, he was a really decent guy, she acknowledged. He wasn't holding spite. He wasn't fretting or doing anything to make her uncomfortable because she had made a decision that he disagreed with and that was a pretty special ability in such a strong and volatile man, wasn't it? But the real problem was, she reckoned, as she watched him leave the room, tall and dark and totally, breathtakingly gorgeous, that the situation they were in would be much easier for her if he behaved badly and made her hate him a little more.

Over the remainder of the week Leo continued to confound her innately low expectations of the male sex. He joined her for a rather windblown picnic on the beach with the children and played ball with Cosmo, who shrieked with excitement and hugged his uncle's knees as if he would never let him go. He read a bedtime story to Popi and even tried a few baby-animal-lost-in-the-jungle noises that made both Popi and Sybella go off into whooping giggles. He was making an effort to spend more time with the children and without being asked or encouraged, finally admitting to her when they were talking about it afterwards that on his own he had felt swamped by the kids and their attention had felt too full-on for him to handle.

Recognising that she was in the mood to offer him sex just for pleasing her, Letty took herself off safely to bed early that night. She also stopped lingering over dinner in the evening when he joined her at the house and made absolutely no comment when he too abandoned the beach house and moved back into his usual room across the corridor from hers. They were discovering a new and *better* way to be with each other, she told herself—friends, partners, whatever anyone wanted to call it. She had wanted more but had had to settle for less, which she could live with perfectly well, she reasoned, noting the dark golden intensity of Leo's eyes with what she assured herself was only academic interest.

The day of the club opening rolled up and Letty spent the afternoon getting ready for her first social appearance as Leo's wife. She was keen to look the part. Her maid did her hair for her, straightening it into a luxuriously conditioned smooth blonde mane and Letty knew that it had never looked that good in her life before. She had ordered cosmetics online and boned up on eye shadow application and she made a major effort there too, before donning the scarlet dress and sliding her feet into the sort of very high heels she had always laughed about. All for Leo, a snide little voice whispered at the back of her head and she ignored the voice, telling herself that presenting herself polished up occasionally was only what her position as Leo's wife demanded.

As she had promised, Letty stepped into the girls' bedroom to show them her dress.

'You look pretty, Mummy Letty,' Popi pronounced, bouncing on top of her bed in her pyjamas and failing to notice how Letty momentarily froze at that designation, tears burning the back of her eyes at the compliment.

'Mummy Letty,' Sybella repeated obediently.

Leo watched Letty come downstairs and immediately regretted choosing the dress because she looked fantastic and incredibly sexy in it and he was tempted enough without the sight of her superb breasts showcased in red and her shapely legs on show. The pulse at his groin which rarely quit around Letty kicked up into a dull throb and he ground his teeth together.

'You look amazing,' Leo murmured hoarsely. 'But you forgot your jewellery…'

'I have my rings on.'

He urged her into his office and opened a big wooden box, full of smaller boxes and a tangled array of other gold and jewels untidily stored. 'My mother's collection. It's all yours to wear now. I would suggest the rubies with that dress.'

Letty stood still as Leo attached a ruby pendant to her throat and handed her earrings to put on. When he was this close and she could smell the wonderfully familiar scent of him she felt light-headed and she gulped in steadying air as she donned the earrings. Leo handed her a gold watch.

'My goodness,' she muttered uneasily. 'I'll look like a Christmas tree.'

'No, you'll look like a Romanos wife...*my* wife,' Leo completed with distinct pride as he removed a ruby and diamond bangle from its protective box and watched her slide it over her hand.

Letty allowed him to escort her out to the helicopter waiting for them before sharing with him that Popi had called her 'Mummy Letty'.

'That's wonderful!' Leo exclaimed with his brilliant flashing smile before he lifted her into the helicopter. 'They've accepted you.'

Letty thought it was rather more of a first step on that road but she didn't deflate him. Loving the children had come as easily to her as loving her own family. Her mother had made a really good recovery from her surgery and was no longer in pain. The boys were back home from their father's as well and everyone was missing her. Popi started back to school after half-term the following week, so she would be back in London soon enough, she reminded herself wryly.

Infinity, Leo's new club in Athens, was surrounded by paparazzi and Leo strode down the red carpet between the crash barriers restraining the crowds, past the surge of flashing cameras and shouted questions, quite unbothered by the attention, while Letty was tempted to pull her hem down to her ankles and haul her neckline up to her chin but didn't have sufficient fabric to achieve either wish.

As she joined Leo at a crowded table of well-wishers, she asked him if his father had arrived yet and he rolled his eyes at the question. 'No, it'll be another no-show on his part. He often makes promises he doesn't keep,' he admitted wryly.

Leo's cynical attitude to his father's failures in the

paternal field made Letty feel sad for him because *her* mother had always been reliable. His insecure background had most definitely damaged Leo's ability to trust either himself or anyone else but she knew he wouldn't appreciate that information.

As Letty's gaze fell on a familiar face at a nearby table, she stiffened and interrupted Leo to hiss, 'What's Dido doing here? Is she one of your *special* guests?'

Leo froze. 'No, but she's a famous actress. I imagine she got a free ticket from the organisers. The more celebrities that attend, the more headlines the event garners,' he countered drily, closing a hand over hers to guide her over to a more secluded table in the corner.

As she sat down a waiter arrived with a tray carrying a birthday cake and another with a bottle of champagne.

'Happy birthday, Letty,' Leo murmured as the cake was ceremonially sliced and the champagne was uncorked to froth down into glasses. 'I had a gift bought for you, but it no longer seemed appropriate so I had to get creative. As an alternative gift, I'm signing that apartment your mother and brothers are living in over to them,' he said quietly. 'Owning the property will give them a greater feeling of security.'

'Oh, Leo, that's so...*so* generous of you!' Letty gasped and hauled him into a hug, painfully aware of how rigid he remained in her hold and quickly drawing back with the sense that she had crossed a boundary she should've respected. 'But what did you originally buy me?' she prompted, hopelessly curious on that score.

'It was an eternity ring.' Leo grimaced. 'I returned it.'

Disappointment filled her because it had been a personal present and an eternity ring from Leo, the studiously free man, would have been a very satisfying item to wear.

As she fumbled for the right words with which to respond, Dido slid into the seat beside Leo. 'Leo, just the man I've been needing to see!' she carolled in English, before shifting into Greek.

Letty strove to be polite and contrived to drain a glass of champagne and even munch on a slice of cake while Dido, once again, ignored her presence. But by the time her glass was refreshed such restraint was becoming a challenge and anger was stirring like green fire in her gaze because the other woman had, very rudely, broken in on a private moment.

'Get rid of her,' she bit out in Leo's ear. *'Or I will!'*

Leo shot her a startled appraisal and then rose from the table to effectively bring the conversation to an end. 'Excuse me,' he murmured smoothly, long brown fingers capturing Letty's to raise her by his side. 'My wife and I are in the midst of celebrating her birthday...'

CHAPTER NINE

'DON'T YOU EVER, for as long as you live, address me like that again!' Leo launched at Letty in a furious undertone as he tugged her up the spiral staircase in the corner and flung open a door into an office, already occupied by an older man.

'Sorry, Dmitri... I need a private space,' said Leo, and the other man quickly vacated the room to leave them alone.

'I am fed up with your ex-girlfriends swarming like piranha fish around us!' Letty sliced back at Leo. 'They're everywhere we go, demanding your attention!'

Leo regarded her, his anger mysteriously ebbing from his bright golden gaze. 'You're a jealous, possessive woman, *yineka mou*,' he declared, utterly disconcerting Letty as she squared up to him with angrily clenched fists. 'And that is remarkable behaviour from a woman who told me to embrace my sexual freedom and kicked me out of bed!'

'I did *not* kick you out of bed!' Letty fired back at him, still trying to work out when she had lost the plot to the extent that she had blamed Leo for Dido's rudeness and persistence and had literally snarled at him. Her cheeks went red. 'But I am not jealous either.'

Leo stalked forward, crowding her back against the desk. 'You *were* jealous,' he persisted with the most curious edge of satisfaction stamped on his lean, darkly handsome features. 'So, how are you planning to handle me being with these other women you want me to sleep with?'

'Like a trooper!' Letty threw back at him. 'It wouldn't mean anything to me. I'm tough.'

'You may be tough,' conceded Leo, framing her hectically flushed face with two big hands. 'But you *are* a lousy liar! You want me and you don't want to share me. I wouldn't want to share you either because you're mine—'

'Oh, take a hike with the property claim!' Letty advised with acid bite. 'I don't belong to you in any way!'

'Let me *show* you then,' Leo growled, rough and low, crushing her mouth under his with such insistence that her knees went weak, all the fiery intensity that was Leo powering his passionate assault on her tender mouth.

With the unfamiliar knowledge that her temper was out of control, Letty's mind was a whirling turmoil of contrasting reactions. She wanted to slap him but she wanted to kiss him back too, and the liquid heat pooling in her pelvis wouldn't let her push him away. Instead she traded kiss for kiss, hard and fierce and so necessary to her in her current mood that she could not have restrained that desperate need hurtling up through her.

And suddenly Leo was settling her down on the desk, long fingers smoothing up her inner thighs to yank with force at her knickers. And Letty was shocked but *not* outraged, hunger for him driving her, ensuring that she too unconditionally craved the drivingly urgent invasion of his body into hers. She yanked at his tousled black hair as he endeavoured to don protection while she ran her greedy hands below his shirt, over the smooth flexing muscles shifting below her every caress.

'You're driving me insane!' Leo rasped in a tone of raw arousal, his eyes blazing like polished gold ingots set between sweeping black lashes.

He sank into the slick wet welcome of her body with an uninhibited groan of appreciation. The desk creaked under that very physical onslaught. Her body jolted, hot sweet delight laced with savage excitement making her heart hammer and her blood race. With every sinuous twist of his lithe hips he hammered the exact spot inside her that maximised her pleasure. The pressure inside her built and built until it surged up through her in a wild white-knuckle climax that made her cry out his name.

'Would this be the right or the wrong moment to say thank you for sharing your birthday with me?' Leo murmured huskily above her head, still panting to catch his breath from his exertions.

As Leo righted his clothing, Letty leapt off the desk like a scalded cat and discovered her legs were too wobbly to hold her upright. 'It was the champagne,' she muttered between clenched teeth.

'One glass? Even you are not that much of a lightweight. No, finally accept that we have crazy good chemistry together,' Leo asserted without remorse.

And why was she looking for remorse from him? she asked herself fiercely. Of course he had no regrets, having just comprehensively proved that he could break down her barriers and persuade her to do what she had sworn *not* to do. A guilty sense of having failed her own standards afflicted Letty.

'*So* good it's off the charts,' Leo grated, hauling her into his arms, striving to hang onto the advantage he had gained. 'The sex ban isn't going to work for us.'

Letty froze as he brushed her tumbled hair back from her woodenly self-contained face to look down at her. 'It *has* to work,' she parried with an edge of desperation because she didn't know who she was any more, what she was trying to do, why she had let herself down to such an extent, and then she gazed up into Leo's stunning eyes and reeled at the beauty of them set in that lean strong face of his.

In that instant, the stark realisation that in the matter of a few short weeks she had become deeply attached to Leo shattered her. She *loved* him. Of course she found it a challenge to step back and deny what her own mind and body longed to have, that intimate connection which might have been essentially meaningless to a male of Leo's experience and habits, but which meant a great deal more to her. No longer could she deny or wilfully misunderstand the powerful feelings he inspired in her. Earlier, he had been right, and she had been wrong. She *was* jealous of his tribe of exes and admirers. She didn't like seeing him with another woman, didn't like watching another woman command his attention. How petty was that?

Yet being with Leo made her feel stronger, more confident, more individual in more ways than she had words to describe. That was the positive side to loving him while she mentally shook her head over the foolishness that accompanied those same feelings. She had lost her temper over pushy Dido, had been intolerant and idiotically possessive. So, he was right and she was wrong. If this was how she truly felt, how could she ever contrive to live with the knowledge that Leo was having sex with other women? Suddenly she felt as though she had backed herself into a corner and she didn't know how to get out of it again.

'Compromise is not the end of the world,' Leo murmured huskily, pressing an abstracted kiss against her furrowed brow, uncomfortably aware that that clever brain of hers was turning like a clock and probably not in his favour. 'Eventually we'll understand what works best for us. It's too soon to make major decisions about our direction right now.'

Letty gritted her teeth. She was too proud to appreciate Leo being generous enough to offer her a face-saving excuse. 'We'll see,' she muttered flatly. 'We should return to our table.'

Leo fished a comb out of his jacket and tidied her hair and suggested she fix her lipstick. She had never felt as ashamed of herself as she did at that moment when she registered that her inexperience in relationships had sent her rushing down the wrong path. It was an effort to return to the crowds downstairs and smile and chat as though nothing whatsoever had happened while her body still hummed and pulsed from Leo's rawly masculine possession. He had won his point but he wasn't crowing in triumph and she supposed she should be grateful for small mercies.

When they arrived back on the island it was very late and when Darius greeted Leo in Greek and spoke words that etched a look of astonishment on Leo's lean strong face, Letty was sprung out of her drowsiness.

'What's happened?'

'Apparently my father arrived here with a suitcase during the evening. Darius seems to think he's broken up with Katrina, but I find that long-desired event very hard to credit,' Leo mused with a curled lip.

As they entered the hall, Letty headed towards the stairs.

'Where are you going?' Leo questioned.

'I thought that you and your father would appreciate privacy,' Letty said uncertainly. 'I mean, if he's in the midst of a personal crisis…'

'My father and I don't have private or personal conversations,' Leo parried drily, and he closed a hand round hers to turn her back in the direction of the main reception room. 'A wife as a third party is very welcome. Panos can get very emotional.'

The distaste with which Leo admitted that truth about his father spoke volumes to Letty. Leo evidently respected men who concealed their feelings more, but Letty considered that attitude archaic.

As they entered the room the older man leapt to his feet and greeted his son in a flood of distraught Greek, which made Letty wish very much that she had made it up the stairs because it didn't feel right to her to be present at such a meeting when she barely knew Leo's father. Leo replied to him in Greek and in what sounded like a bracing tone but whatever he said etched an expression of grief-stricken horror on Panos's face and he fell back down on the sofa and sobbed as though his heart would break.

'What on earth did you say?' Letty whispered.

'That she's been having affairs for over twenty years,' Leo murmured in an undertone.

'Is that how you would normally comfort someone who's just had their heart broken?' Letty snapped back in disbelief that Leo had chosen that particular moment to drop even worse news on his father about his estranged wife.

'No, but it is essential that he understands *right now* that her betrayal is not an isolated episode which he can forgive or overlook,' Leo proffered without shame.

'I disagree,' said Letty, approaching the older man and ordering some tea and supper for him before sitting down beside him to offer him the compassion that his son appeared to lack.

Yes, even at that point she grasped that Leo and his late sister had suffered as children at his stepmother's unmaternal hands and that, as adults, they and even Ana's children had been shoved out of their father's life at Katrina's behest. And Katrina had even tried to get Leo into bed. She fully understood that Katrina was a nasty corrupt woman, but she also understood that Panos Romanos genuinely loved her and was entitled to sympathetic support from his son, who was, aside of the children, his only surviving family. And what she saw was that Leo was not prepared to offer that support because he despised his father's ongoing attachment to Katrina and the evidence of his grief over the loss of her.

Leo was aware that Letty thought he was being cruel but he knew better. He was being cruel to be kind. Now that Katrina's infidelity was out in the open, it was time to be honest rather than offer empty consolations. Watching his father grip both of Letty's hands and sob out English words, Leo rolled his eyes and walked out of the room. How could he have a father with so little control over his emotions? He cringed inwardly at the thought of ever allowing a woman to bring him down that low. It was shameful, utterly shameful for a man to be so infatuated with a woman that he thought his life was at an end because she had betrayed him. Leo assured himself that he would never descend to such a level of weakness. He didn't *need* any woman and he never would, and seeing his father in such a state only reinforced that warning.

By the time Letty finally contrived to persuade Panos that he needed to go to bed and sleep, it was almost dawn and he had told her the whole story of his two marriages from start to finish. She wished Leo had stayed for those revelations because they might have made him a little less judgemental. If there was one thing she could do for Leo, it would be to persuade him to talk to his father about Leo's mother and what their marriage had been like because Leo had put his mother on a saint's pedestal at the age of six and had made a lot of wrong assumptions about his father. Unfortunately, Leo would probably be very resistant to the idea that there were two sides to every story.

When she entered the bedroom she had been using it was disconcerting for her to meet Leo walking out of the bathroom with only a towel linked round his lean hips. 'Why are you in here?' she queried wearily, too worn out by her hours of comforting Panos to voice it as anything more than a fleetingly curious question.

'We are not sleeping apart any more,' Leo informed her. 'How is he?'

Letty stopped dead. 'Do you actually *care*? I mean, you just walked out and left me with him!' she said bitterly.

'I've been waiting for over twenty years for Katrina to be exposed as the monster she is,' Leo countered unapologetically. 'Her infidelity was widely known. She made my father a laughing stock and the only reason I didn't intervene and tell him the truth about her sooner was that she made him happy and I didn't want to be the messenger. Forgive me if I find it too much of a challenge to cry crocodile tears over the reality that she's now going to become his ex-wife.'

'You need to talk to your father about his marriage to your mother. You need to hear what that was like.'

'Who the hell do you think you are to drag my mother into this sordid situation?' Leo launched at her, wholly taken aback by that advice.

'Someone who, thanks to your walk-out tonight, knows rather more than I feel I should about your background,' Letty observed heavily. 'Seriously, Leo. You need to get over yourself and talk to your dad.'

Leo stiffened defensively. 'It's not a matter of getting over myself—'

'No, it's a matter of setting aside your prejudice and taking a fresh look at old history—'

'You could simply just tell me what he told you,' Leo stated impatiently.

'No. It's not my business,' Letty said succinctly. 'It's father and son stuff. And now I'm going to bed and I'm going to sleep for hours.'

Leo was transfixed by that little conversation while cursing Letty's sense of honour in feeling that it was not her place to share such stuff with him second-hand because he had never had a personal chat with his father in his entire life and he wasn't looking forward to the prospect. How would he even approach such a challenge? Curiosity, however, was pulling at him.

'Letty's wonderful,' his father assured him over lunch, when he came downstairs. 'An amazing woman. So kind and thoughtful and loving. You're very lucky.'

Leo ordered coffee on the veranda and sat down there with his father for the first time in many years. Panos still looked worn, his eyes bloodshot, his weathered face still puffy from his distress the night before. Leo was seriously hoping that he didn't start crying again because he didn't think he would cope very well with that but, now that the truth about Katrina was finally out, he was learning that he *did* feel more sympathetic towards his father's plight than he had ever imagined he would.

Panos explained how, having missed his flight to Athens, he had returned unexpectedly to the hotel, where he had discovered Katrina in bed with one of Leo and Letty's wedding guests. Leo nodded and answered his father's questions about why he had remained silent for so long about Katrina's affairs. Leo gave him the honest answer and went on to ask the kind of questions about his mother that it had never even occurred to him to ask before. And what he learned then rocked his world and his perceptions about his family. He discovered then that he *could* handle the tears shining in the older man's eyes. He discovered that those tears didn't seem so weak once he was better aware of Panos's experiences. He also appreciated that he owed his bride enormous gratitude for pushing him into that long-overdue dialogue with his only surviving parent.

For that reason, when Letty finally reappeared, surrounded by leaping, jumping kids and with Theon tucked securely on one hip, Leo experienced one of those increasingly rare moments when he wished there were no children in his life because he wanted Letty all to himself and he couldn't have her. Even his father gravitated straight to her as though drawn by the magnet of her warmth and smiles. Leo wanted those smiles all to himself, he registered in surprise at that acknowledgement.

Over dinner, Letty rifled through the letters that had arrived that day for her and extracted one that provoked a huge grin from her. 'I've got an interview next week,' she told him.

Leo frowned. 'For what?'

'To return to medical school,' Letty replied happily. 'I've applied for entrance for next year because I thought the kids and I should have the rest of this year to bond.'

Leo wondered when *he* would get the chance to bond with her and then questioned why he was having such a weird thought when they were already married. 'I'm sure they'll rearrange the interview for you,' he commented.

Letty frowned. 'There's no need to rearrange it. Popi returns to school next week, so it all dovetails perfectly.'

'Popi can return to London with one of the nannies and the rest of the kids while you stay on here. I have meetings in Athens next week,' Leo pointed out equably, certain he had found the perfect solution.

Letty wrinkled her nose. 'Oh, that won't do. We

can't separate the children and Popi shouldn't be in that huge house alone.'

'Alone with a domestic staff of at least ten people,' Leo slotted in drily, wishing yet again that Letty didn't place literally everyone else's needs ahead of his. '*I want you to stay here with me next week.*'

Letty opened and closed her mouth a couple of times and then encountered her father-in-law's curious gaze and opted to remain silent. She would talk to Leo in private, *fight* with him without an audience because she had not the slightest doubt that it would be a fight when Leo spoke in that *my way or the highway* measured tone.

'Leo...?' she murmured from the office doorway once the children were in bed and his father had gone down to the village to catch up with old friends.

Leo frowned down at his laptop and then glanced up, immediately thinking how incredibly beautiful she was, even in worn jeans and a sweater. Maybe it was the appeal of *au naturel* to a man who had never had that option with a woman before, he reasoned absently. There was faint colour in her cheeks and with her hair tumbling round her shoulders just a little messily she still contrived to look amazingly appealing to his eyes, and thinking about that wildly sensual little encounter in his manager's office made him instantly hard.

'Yes?' His voice emerged huskily.

'I have to return to London next week and I'm taking all the kids as well,' Letty told him bluntly.

Leo frowned. 'But I'd prefer you to remain here with me.'

Letty drew in a deep breath. 'Leo...you married me to be a mother figure to the children, so please allow me to occasionally know what's best for them. Popi would be upset to be parted from her sister and brothers and I want to attend that interview, *not* rearrange it. Don't forget that my right to return to studying medicine is in our prenup.'

All of a sudden Leo could feel his usually very even and controlled temper threatening to go nuclear on him. He realised that it was her reference to that wretched prenuptial agreement that set him off, not to mention his father's disturbing revelations about his marriage to Leo's mother. Had the document been sitting in front of him at that moment he would have ripped it to shreds. 'Does that mean you can't compromise?' he pressed in a curt undertone.

'I won't compromise when it comes to being straight about what the children need,' Letty countered squarely. 'I'm sorry, that's not something that can be or should be negotiated.'

Leo released his breath on a long slow hiss and vaulted upright. Stunning dark golden eyes locked to her like grappling hooks. 'We're newly married. I am *trying* to be reasonable here!' he bit out in a harsh undertone. 'I want you to make what I want a priority— your *main* priority.'

Letty suppressed a sigh and cursed all the very many willing-to-please women who had worked tirelessly together to imbue Leo, the ultimate Greek tycoon, with such an outdated set of values. 'This time I'm going to say no because the children are still too vulnerable to suffer separation or too much disruption…but another time, when they are better adjusted to their life with us, I *will* try to accommodate your wishes.'

Leo ground his teeth together. He totally understood

her reasoning, even sympathised, but they had been married only a week and had spent very little time together. Now they would be apart another week and soon after that he had a trip to the US planned. Exactly when was he going to find time to *be* with his wife? Surely that should be of crucial importance to her too because without a functioning marriage, where would the children be then?

Feeling very dissatisfied with Leo's reaction, Letty went off to dig out a book and read while striving to put that exchange behind her and not brood. She had to be reasonable, she instructed herself. She was dealing with a pretty spoilt and selfish man, who was still learning to deal with the changes children brought to life. Leo wasn't likely to turn into a gilded saint overnight and her constantly reminding him that the kids had to come first seemed to be a particular goad. She wondered why that was when he had only married her to be their substitute mother.

She was tossing and turning, sleepless and still trying to fathom the mystery that was Leo's tangled and contradictory thought processes, when Leo slid into bed beside her, startling her. 'I thought you were still working,' she commented.

'No. I need to make the most of my wife while she's still here and available,' Leo told her, stripping her out of her silky nightgown with ruthless efficiency.

Rather exciting efficiency, Letty conceded, pulses picking up speed, heart pounding before his mouth even enclosed hers. She lifted up to him, wildly enthralled by the lean, hard muscular length of him pressing down on her. She was learning so much about herself that her head was spinning, registering that even when Leo set her teeth on edge she continued to crave him and was reassured now rather than annoyed to find herself still an object of desire. She loved him so much, she thought passionately, small fingers smoothing caressingly over his satin-smooth broad shoulders and up into his silky hair. There was no rhyme or reason to it but Leo was *it* for her, the summit of her dreams, her most insane fantasies and the key to her happiness and accepting that reality unnerved her a little.

'Get with the programme,' Leo breathed, gazing down at her with eyes that glittered jet black in the moonlight. 'You're a thousand miles away inside your head.'

'How do you know that?' Letty asked with a look of guilt.

'Because you're the only woman who has ever treated me like that and it is *not* a compliment,' he murmured ruefully.

'Well, maybe I'm disconnecting because you're always in control,' Letty suggested, planting her hands against his chest and sending him flat on the mattress beside her because she was embarrassed by the truth that she had floated away inside her anxious thoughts.

Letty revelled in Leo's surprise and she chuckled. 'So lie back and think of Greece like Victorian women used to do—'

Obligingly, Leo stretched, naked and bronzed and awesomely attractive, all lithe and sexy and willing to be seduced. Letty grinned down at him. 'Now, I warn you I may be a little clumsy at first, but practice is crucial,' she pointed out.

Leo lay back and surveyed the wonder that was Letty, who never ever did anything the way he expected and, as he was discovering, it was an extraordinarily fascinating quality in a woman. He had been seduced by women to whom sex was an art form, but every stroke of Letty's uncertain fingers, every tiny enthusiastic kiss from her generous mouth had an infinitely stronger effect on him. And whether it was the medical training or the truth that he had married a superbly sensual woman, it was the sexiest hour he had ever enjoyed, and he told her so afterwards.

'Nonsense,' she told him, a little crossly because he had stopped her at what she considered to be a crucial point and before he could climax and she felt cheated.

Leo spread her out across the bed. 'Now it's my turn.'

He found her ready, *aching* for him, and he plunged and she gasped in delight at the sheer rush of sensation flaring and flaming through her needy body. She wanted more and he gave her more until containing that pleasure became too much and she rose against him with a keening cry as sweet gratification flooded her in an unstoppable rush.

'You will miss me when you're in London, *meli mou*,' Leo pronounced with satisfaction.

And Letty saw no good reason to deny the truth because sometimes that was just the way the cookie crumbled. 'Yes, but life throws you lemons occasionally when you really want peaches.'

Leo laughed out loud in appreciation and held her close because he was already thinking of round two.

And she lay there, feeling unexpectedly secure and happy, thinking *I can do this*.

CHAPTER TEN

LEO WATCHED IN near disbelief as his father climbed into the helicopter with the children, the nannies and Letty: *he* was going to London too.

Letty had invited Panos, pointing out to Leo that the grandkids were a great source of distraction for the older man and that, apparently, *he* enjoyed Christmas shopping. And, seemingly, she planned to be doing a great deal of shopping, even though it was only November and Christmas had never started for Leo before Christmas Eve, when a last-minute dash settled all his requirements.

'But I've got so many people to buy for now and no credit limit!' Letty had enthused with starry eyes and not a hint of the greed Leo was accustomed to seeing in a woman's face. He knew that Letty was already imagining the pleasure she could give to others with her gifts and he frowned at that oddity and yet smiled at the same time.

Even so, his entire family abandoning him sucked, Leo conceded grimly. Like rats leaving a sinking ship, they had left him alone, the wagons circling Letty as though she were a bonfire on a winter's day. A text arrived on his phone and he glanced down at it, his jawline hardening as he recognised that he had a small problem from his more eventful past that required handling…and not with gracious tact either.

In the week that followed, Leo had a great deal to think about because he was still coming to terms with what his father had confessed about his marriage to Leo's mother, Athena. Having his assumptions about both parents so brutally rearranged had shaken Leo, reminding him that he had been a clueless six-year-old when his mother, Athena, died, giving birth to his sister, Ana.

Athena had been an extremely wealthy heiress, an only child of the Romanos dynasty with an authoritarian widowed father. Part of the marriage settlement had entailed Panos's agreement to assume the Romanos name on the marriage. On their wedding night Athena had admitted that she had only married Panos because her father had threatened to disinherit her in favour of his nephew if she did not marry and have a child. She had also disclosed the truth that, having been abused as a little girl by a long-dead uncle, she had no interest in sex but would engage in it solely to conceive as she too longed to have a child of her own. Leo's father had been urged to seek sexual pleasure elsewhere by his bride.

Learning those facts had utterly transformed Leo's image of his father, whom he had long tended to view rather as a fortune-hunting adulterous gigolo who had taken advantage of a naïve heiress. Ironically, if anything, it was his *father* who had suffered rejection from the woman he'd loved and who had continued to love the troubled woman until she died.

Katrina had come *after* Athena's death, *not* before, as Leo had always believed and his father, overwhelmed to find himself apparently wanted and loved at last, had fallen fast and hard and had swiftly remarried, hoping for a more normal marriage. By the end of that admission, Leo had sympathised with the older man, understanding, as Panos did not, that he had been targeted by Katrina, who had assumed he was much richer than he truly was. The family trust had ensured that Athena's children inherited virtually everything that had been hers, limiting his father to only an ongoing income from the estate while he was raising his two children and, after that, a considerably smaller income.

In short, Leo was suffering a great deal of regret when it came to his father. Panos had been stitched up in the marriage settlement by Leo's wily grandfather, duped into his first marriage and had then fallen madly in love with a mercenary and unscrupulous woman. Yet Leo had never reached out to the older man and had never offered him financial help, had, effectively, never done anything but judge on false premises and found Panos wanting. That awareness sat on his conscience like a giant weight and he would have liked to discuss it with Letty, only she wasn't there and the wretched house echoed with her absence…

In contrast to Leo, Letty, *initially*, had a wonderful time back in London. She enjoyed a most successful interview relating to her return to medical school and was assured of her place the following year. Her mother was slowly becoming fully mobile again and it had transformed her life. She was ready to return to being the active, interested parent whom Letty recalled from her younger years and she was quite overpowered by Leo's generous signing over of the lovely apartment, where she was now living in comfort. It was a challenge for Gillian to grasp the extent of the Romanos wealth but a visit to her daughter's marital home in London helped to dispel her misapprehension that her son-in-law had spent money he couldn't afford to spend on her.

Her half-brothers, on the other hand, had converted to their new lifestyle with an enthusiasm that was slightly embarrassing to Letty, but the sight of Leo's games room in the mansion provoked them into excited whoops of rare teenage enthusiasm. Assured that her family's future was now rosy beyond belief from what it had been only weeks earlier, Letty could only be happy at what her marriage had achieved for those she loved.

Panos, meanwhile, had found a compassionate listener in her mother, Gillian, because both of them had suffered the misery of having an unfaithful partner. At the same time, Panos, having recovered from the first shock of Katrina's betrayal, was already moving on and was very much occupied getting to know the grandchildren that Katrina had rigorously kept him apart from to finally become a loving grandfather to his daughter's orphaned offspring. He had also admitted to Letty that his new closeness to Leo meant a great deal to him because Leo's reserve had kept him at a distance for years.

In the meantime, Letty was resisting Popi's pleas to put up Christmas decorations in November, so excited was the little girl at the prospect of the festive season. Apparently, her late mother, Ana, had always done so and Letty was tempted but stood firm on the point until Gillian shoved a gossip page under her nose when they were having coffee one morning, ten days after her return to London.

'I think it's sickening what these journalists try to do to rich men like Leo!' Letty's mother opined in disgust. 'There he is, having a business lunch or a meal with a friend, and they try to make it into something sordid just to get a story!'

Letty glanced down at the black and white photo of Leo caught in profile, smiling at the woman on the other side of the table, and her breath caught in her throat because it was Dido, the beautiful actress who had pursued Leo with such relentless interest on the two occasions when she had met her.

'She's an old flame,' she said and for her mother's benefit she forced her shoulders into a careless shrug and smiled, keen to hide that she felt as though someone had just planted a knife in her heart. She understood from her mother's face that she was genuinely worried that her daughter had married a man who slept around, just as her ex-husband had.

'Oh...' Gillian responded uncomfortably, searching her daughter's expression for any sign of concern. 'But you don't think *that*—?'

'No, of course not!' That was when Letty's previously unexercised acting ability really kicked in and she contrived to laugh to reassure the older woman. '*Not* Leo,' she declared firmly. 'He's not like Robbie in any way.'

'I didn't think so,' Gillian agreed with clear relief on her daughter's behalf. 'You wouldn't stand for that.'

'No, I wouldn't,' Letty fibbed with a frog in her throat and a fierce attempt to hold back the shocked tears stinging the back of her eyes as she thought about that prenuptial agreement and Leo's determination to keep it in place.

Well, Leo had *warned* her, hadn't he? Really, why was she so shocked by what had been written in the stars, never mind imposed in legal terms, even *before* they'd married?

Panos wandered in to join the women and Letty took the opportunity to make an excuse and leave the older couple chatting. Inside her chest she could feel her heart cracking down the middle and she went into the bathroom she had been naively expecting to share with Leo as a couple, closed the door and broke down into sobbing misery.

She would allow herself thirty minutes in which to grieve the loss of hope and faith which she had just endured. Leo had been with Dido and no way could she credit that it had been innocent when she was aware that the actress was so desperate to regain his interest. Dido was the sort of woman always ready to pounce on an available man and, evidently, Leo *was* still available. He had been unfaithful to her, exactly as she had feared. *Deal with it*, she told herself fiercely…but *how*?

She needed to protect herself, needed to be strong and, ironically, being with Leo, living with Leo and challenging him *had* made her stronger, she acknowledged wryly. She was tough as old boots, she told herself; she could do it.

After all, nothing had gone the way she had expected in their marriage. First, they had been in agreement that their marriage would be sexless and then Leo had changed his mind and changed her mind as well. She had then swung back on the defensive once she'd appreciated that Leo was still not willing to surrender his freedom to sleep with whomever he chose. For the space of a week they had been extremely polite to each other, but that week had concluded with her breaking her promise to herself that he *had* to remain faithful and she was now thinking of that thoroughly wanton joining on the office desk of Leo's new club. Recalling that episode her face burned, and it burned even more when she looked back on the sensual indulgence of that last week she had spent on the island with Leo.

They had been like rabbits, she thought shamefacedly, her entire body tightening and heating in acknowledgement of her own weakness. *She* hadn't been able to keep her hands off him. It was not as though Leo had been sex-starved at the time of her departure, it was not as though there were any kind of excuse for his meeting up with Dido again. Maybe there *was* such a thing as sex addiction, the celebrity excuse for misbehaviour, but the suggestion of rehabilitation wasn't one she felt equal to tackling with Leo. He would probably just laugh, she reflected, stricken, because evidently he saw sexual freedom as one of life's necessities and he was determined not to live any other way.

And that was the guy she had *knowingly* married and fallen crazily in love with, she reminded herself with dogged honesty. He had been upfront on the fidelity score from the very beginning.

Her head was starting to ache and she checked herself in the mirror, appalled to see how red her nose was and how swollen her eyes were from her giving way so freely to her distress. Yes, thirty minutes of self-pity was all she would allow herself for hadn't she agreed to the marriage? And wasn't she very happy with what that marriage had achieved for her family?

Yes, she was.

And if she divorced Leo she would lose the children and she loved them too. Occasional access to Popi, Sybella, Cosmo and Theon would not compensate any of them for such a brutal severance. The children would suffer, and she did not have an automatic right to write off their need for her as a mother simply because marriage to Leo was turning out to be more of a nightmare than she had innocently foreseen.

Life wasn't that simple, she acknowledged ruefully. The innocents in her family and his would be hurt by her departure from Leo's life. If she broke up with Leo, her mother would want to sell the apartment she lived in and return the money to him because that was the sort of woman she was. Accepting such a massive gift from a member of her family, as Leo currently was, was one thing but retaining it as the proceeds of a very short-lived marriage would strike Gillian as something else entirely.

So, she had to be tough and adapt to being married to an adulterous husband, didn't she? She would *stay* married to Leo. She would hide her hurt and act as if everything in the garden was rosy and wonderful because only then could she keep everybody around her happy.

Her eyes misted again just when she was managing to use concealer on her eyes and she blinked rapidly. On one level she didn't want to live like that but just then she didn't feel she had much of a choice unless she was prepared to destroy everything that their marriage had achieved…

And just as Panos had required a distraction from his depressed thoughts about his broken marriage,

Letty registered that she needed one too. Leo phoned her every day and while, only hours ago, she had been longing for his arrival in London, now she was considering it fortunate that it would be a couple of weeks before he returned. His absence would give her time to come to terms with his infidelity in whatever way she could, and she had to stop loving and missing him as well because that was an even worse recipe for disaster and she would have to live in a continual state of being hurt and disillusioned.

So, step one in her own necessary emotional rehabilitation, she told herself in her mirror reflection, was to *stop* loving Leo, step back, *look after herself...* That was the sensible approach.

By the time she was descending the stairs it was lunchtime, Leo's father and her mother were still chatting and Popi was home from school, proudly displaying a homemade Christmas card with drawings of her family that made Letty crack up in genuine appreciation. Ana's children were learning to see her and Leo as their family unit and she was proud of that achievement and resolved not to damage it with what she told herself would be selfish oversensitivity. She would cope with his infidelity because she was tough, she reminded herself doggedly, but she wouldn't continue to sleep with him. They would have the convenient marriage he had first wanted while she devoted herself to raising the children and completing her studies. That way she would preserve her dignity and her strength.

As for the distraction she sensed she currently needed while she came to terms with the effective end of her intimacy with Leo, she decided to go for an over-the-top Christmas to delight the children and keep herself busy. Christmas was going to start in November for them, just as it had when they had still had their birthparents. And she was going to buy a family dog and buy a present for Leo, even though he didn't deserve one. Yes, she would be treating him perfectly normally by the time he flew back from the US, doubtless having sampled various other female bodies during his time away from her, she told herself sourly. He would not even suspect that anything was amiss with her. She would be solid steel and calm and quite unbothered by what she had discovered...

Leo arrived home on the first day of December and so unrecognisable was his home he almost walked straight out of the door again. A scruffy terrier rushed up to him, sniffed him thoroughly and then retreated to bark as though he were an intruder. That was odd enough, but the transformation of the entrance hall could only put him in mind of a Christmas grotto gone mad. There was not an inch of space left because everywhere he looked there were glittering trees, giant stuffed reindeer and elves, stockings and tinsel and holly and decorations. A log fire roared in the grate of a fireplace that had never been lit before. He had vague memories of his sister's house during the festive season but even his kid sister, bless her heart, hadn't gone for anything quite so magnificent or...extreme.

Leo smiled though, registering that Letty treated Christmas as an explosion of glitter and good cheer, which was probably exactly what the children loved. He did notice the absence of mistletoe though, just as he noticed that the warm welcome he had subconsciously expected from his wife was missing. At that point the children came rushing downstairs and he was greeted with all the enthusiasm he could've wished for, attended by cries of 'Unc' Leo' and 'Daddy Leo', because evidently the children hadn't yet made up their minds what to call him.

Of course, all his conversations with Letty on the phone had somehow always turned into conversations about the children. No matter how hard he had tried to take those talks in a more personal direction, he had been redirected to discussing his nephews and nieces. The whole time he was away he had felt starved of Letty, as if she was a presence that could only be pinned down and enjoyed when she was face to face with him. He had sensed the difference in her attitude towards him; he did not consider himself an imaginative man and it bothered him, seriously disturbed his usual rock-solid assurance with women. Something was badly wrong with Letty and that brought him out in a cold sweat of anxiety that he had never experienced before.

'Where's Letty?' he asked with a rather fake smile when his father and mother-in-law appeared in the doorway of the drawing room.

'She had to rush out for something and she took Theon with her,' Gillian imparted anxiously. 'I did warn her that she might miss you but she's got *so* into this Christmas stuff—'

'It's wonderful that she has,' Leo commented, not having failed to notice that he had three happy kids bouncing and chattering at his side when only months earlier they had all been subdued and tense. 'How are you doing, Dad?'

'Oh, I'm feeling much more myself,' Panos Romanos assured him with a grin and a hand that Leo noted, surprisingly, had been anchored on Gillian's slim hip. 'Friends and family, that's what my life is all about now.'

Bit more than friends, Leo reckoned by the very sociable way the older couple kept on exchanging glances. 'I'm disappointed Letty's not here,' he admitted. 'I mean, I've been gone for weeks and—'

The front door opened, and Letty blew in with the baby clamped to one hip. 'Leo, I'm so sorry I wasn't here!' she carolled because their respective parents were standing there as an audience and she didn't want either of them to suspect that anything was amiss between her and Leo.

Passing over Theon to the nanny at the foot of the stairs, whereupon he wailed like a banshee in protest, Letty stripped off her coat and gloves and feasted her attention on Leo. Still absolutely gorgeous, clad in a cashmere overcoat on top of one of his exquisitely well-fitted business suits, he *still* took her breath away. That was a disappointment, she allowed, because she had tried to make him less sexy in her recollections, worked hard at trying to make herself less vulnerable. But there he stood and even travel-worn and badly in need of a shave, stubble outlining his wide sensual mouth and somehow accentuating his fantastic bone structure and oh, those eyes... Well, they certainly weren't the windows of the soul, she scolded herself. His eyes were spectacular but they had to carry a hint of an innately manipulative and secretive personality, she instructed herself. After all, this was the man she had spent pretty much most of a week in bed with, striving to be the sensual woman every man was supposed to want and crave…and where had it got her?

Well, he had given her a great deal of sexual satisfaction and then he had still gone on to get into bed with other women. Oh, yes, she was convinced that there had been *more* than that encounter with Dido, for the opportunities to flirt and seduce for a man of Leo's looks and wealth probably came up everywhere he went, particularly when he was travelling. This was a guy she literally could not trust out of her sight, she reminded herself sternly.

'So, how was your trip?' Letty asked Leo with an interest that even he could see was false, for she was not a good dissembler and her expressive face was a dead giveaway.

'Like every other trip.'

What the hell had he done? Leo was asking himself in frustration, striving to think of something he might have said on the phone that could have brought about such a change in her. She had left Ios acting warm and confiding and caring and all of a sudden that was gone. He watched in disbelief as Letty sped upstairs, clearly keen to leave him behind, and that was the final straw that broke his control and sent him stalking up the stairs in her wake.

Letty was locked in the bathroom, frantically washing and rewashing her hands, unaware that she was doing it while she struggled to work out how she was supposed to deal with Leo, now that he was back in the house.

She had decorated the whole house for Christmas. There were trees everywhere but the bedrooms. They now had George the dog, a rescue animal with more bad habits than a criminal. George chewed everything from shoes to rugs. He stole food. He tried to get into bed with the children. Much like Leo, George had no boundaries but, unlike Leo, he was very loving. Leo would totally freak out if he knew she was comparing him, even in passing, with a homeless animal, she conceded, finally drying her hands and pulling herself together, although the tendency to cry over the pain she was suppressing still hovered over her like a threatening black cloud. It had been easier to pretend to be happy when Leo was absent. Now that he was back it was a huge challenge for her.

'Letty!' A sharp knock sounded on the door and she froze like a burglar caught in the act of theft before swallowing hard and opening the door.

'Sorry… I'm sure you want a shower,' she said in a brittle tone.

'No, surprisingly enough,' Leo murmured with only the merest hint of sarcasm, 'I wanted to see my wife.'

Halfway to the bedroom door to leave, Letty stilled. *'Oh?'* she said, spinning reluctantly back.

'Luckily for me, you are a lousy actress,' Leo continued tautly, subjecting her to a feverishly intense scrutiny. 'I'm not blind, Letty. What's wrong? Obviously there's something wrong because you've *changed*.'

Letty lost colour and stiffened, wondering how on earth he had so quickly registered that change on her part while she had flattered herself with the belief that she was treating him as she always had.

'We've always been honest with each other,' Leo bit out harshly in the dragging silence that had fallen between them.

'I saw a newspaper photo of you having lunch with

Dido,' Letty framed flatly, accusingly, failing utterly to hold back that tone of condemnation. 'I didn't require anything else to know that you'd returned to your former way of life.'

'*Theé mou*, Letty,' Leo growled. 'I'm not guilty of that cardinal error. I lunched with Dido, no argument on that score. For a long time I've been a theatre angel. I back stage productions that are likely to be successful. That's how I first met Dido years ago. She was a very good investment.'

'Investment?' Letty echoed with raised brows and a frown. 'I think your ties were rather more intimate than that.'

'*Were* being the correct word. Eight years ago, Letty, and there has been no sexual intimacy between us since that ended after an affair that lasted a couple of months,' Leo clarified. 'Dido, who is fiercely ambitious, chases me purely for my wealth in the hope of persuading me to invest in her next stage production. But, to be frank, I only had lunch with her in the first place to tell her to back off with the texts and the allegedly accidental meetings and the pretence that we were once a couple. We were never a couple. We were never close…and that's the truth.'

Letty clamped her hands together because they were trembling, and she didn't want him to notice that humiliating fact. 'I'm not sure I can believe—'

'I'm afraid you *have* to because I will not accept that one stupid photo can come between you and me!' Leo countered in a raw undertone.

'No…' Letty made an almost clumsy movement with one hand to express her continuing tension. 'What came between us was your insistence on retaining your freedom as a married man, which meant that naturally when I saw you in company with Dido, I assumed—'

Leo cast off his coat and dug a hand into the inner pocket of his suit jacket to withdraw a folded document. 'Our prenuptial agreement with that clause removed. You have to sign it too with a witness before it's legal but please note the date when I signed...'

Her throat tight, her brow indented with uncertainty as she accepted the document and rifled through it to check that the that offensive clause had genuinely been removed and not simply rephrased and slipped in some-place else. He had signed it within a day of her leaving the island, which was a surprise.

As Letty sat down at the foot of the bed to read it all properly, Leo's mouth quirked with appreciation. 'You're never going to take me on trust, are you?'

'Probably not,' she agreed, setting the prenuptial contract down beside her on the bed and adding, 'So... I have to ask...what led to this sudden change of heart. I mean, I know that only a few days before you signed that you were still vehemently insisting that you had to keep that freedom.'

Put on the spot that directly, Leo grimaced. 'Find-ing out what my father went through, married to my mother, had an enormous effect on me. It knocked me for six,' he confessed with faint embarrassment. 'I have ignored him pretty much all my life because I held onto unfair assumptions about his character but, when I re-ally thought about it, my resentment came down to his inability to control Katrina and the way she treated my sister and me as children. I blamed him for that because *he* married her. Now I appreciate that he had no idea what was going on in his own home because she never treated us badly when he was around.'

Letty nodded. 'You had a real heart to heart with him, didn't you?' she pressed.

'And I have you to thank for that because without your intervention I would have gone on with the same mind-set.' He sighed with regret. 'Now I have the father I always wanted but didn't appreciate. Katrina being gone from our lives makes that possible.'

'Does he *know*…? I mean, about Katrina coming on to you as well?' Letty enquired with a grimace of distaste.

'Yes. There had to be total honesty from both of us. He was devastated when I told him, but I think it also helped him to accept that Katrina never loved him the way he believed she did and, in a sense, it drew a line under all the rest of it,' he completed grimly. 'I notice that his state of mind is much improved since I last saw him.'

'Yes, Mum and he are great buddies,' Letty remarked. 'I understand everything that you're sharing with me but I still don't understand why you finally decided to remove that clause from the agreement. Just to please me? To lull me into a false sense of security? Why?'

'Do you believe me about Dido? She was after my financial backing, not me personally,' Leo stated in frustration. 'She's very persistent, and I realised that it would take a personal meeting and a blunt refusal to get her to back off. She's so vain that she couldn't see that flattery and flirtation weren't going to get her anywhere with me, particularly after she had offended my wife. That's what that lunch was about.'

Letty nodded, wryly amused at that 'offended my wife', thrown in as if it was a fact of life that Leo should object to such a sin. 'Yes, I believe that the lunch was innocent,' she conceded, feeling a great rolling wave of wounded pain evaporating from her stiff body as she sat there. 'So, according to you, you're going to be faithful now...or are you still in the *trying* to be faithful phase?' she asked suspiciously.

'No, I'm all yours, *entirely* yours,' Leo stressed, a faint smile lightening the lingering strain etched around his wide sensual mouth. 'For good.'

Letty frowned. *'For good?'* she queried in astonishment.

'You're not grasping what I'm trying to tell you here, *yineka mou*,' Leo lamented. 'A gorgeous blonde in biker leathers came into my office and blew my whole life apart in the space of a day. Within a week I was more fascinated by her than any woman I have ever met. Within two weeks I was so hot for her I was performing mental acrobatics to persuade her into being mine, *really* mine...but I hadn't quite come to terms with what I was signing up for. That was my mistake. I came at you like a bull in a china shop *before* I had thought it all through.'

'Are you talking about me?' Letty whispered uncertainly.

'Letty, who the hell else would I be talking about?' he groaned, crouching down in front of her. 'When I said I'm yours for good, I was telling you that I fell head over heels in love with you like a stupid teenager.'

Her lashes fluttered up on wide green eyes as she studied him fixedly. 'Like a very bright but emotionally stunted teenager,' she parried.

'I knew you would put another spin on it…so to try romance with an unromantic and very practical woman and me being a man who has never tried that before either,' Leo admitted ruefully, 'I bought *this*…'

In a state of disbelief at Leo telling her that he had fallen in love with her, Letty watched as he threaded a diamond eternity ring on her finger next to her wedding band. 'Is that the one I *didn't* get for my birthday?' she asked uneasily.

'No, it's an entirely new and much more expensive one and this time it truly expresses what I feel—that I've got to have you for ever,' Leo confessed.

'Oh…' Letty was speechless, plunged in the misery of believing she was being forced to welcome home an unfaithful husband and then sent shooting back up to heights she had never dared to even dream of, before being told that she was loved. Leo *loved* her. It felt as if she was living a dream, a dizzy impossible girlish dream, and she burst into floods of tears, her self-control destroyed.

'*Theós mou*…what did I say?' Leo exclaimed, vaulting back upright again and hauling her up into the circle of his arms.

'I'm just so h-happy!' Letty sobbed into his shoulder. 'I was worried you were a sex addict rather than a player and I didn't think you'd consider therapy—'

'Listen to me for once. I was never a player. I never did one-night stands. I picked one woman and would be with her for a couple of months…a mistress, rather than a lover, though,' Leo hastened to explain.

'But why…*mistresses*?' Letty demanded, struggling to get the stupid, far too emotional, tears back under control because she knew he had to think she was crazy to react like that to a declaration of love.

'Think about it, Letty. I never knew love. When I was still pretty young my grandfather informed me that I would be expected to marry but that the men in my family always had mistresses. It was what he called "a tidy solution". He had one. I assumed my father had one, although he assures me he didn't. It seemed normal not to want to get involved, other than sexually, with a woman. My mother's love is the vaguest, most distant memory. My stepmother had no time for me and I soon understood that she didn't love my father either,' he explained. 'Although Panos tried to be affectionate I backed away from it because Katrina was worse if Ana or I took my father's attention away from her. I didn't know what love was. I didn't know what it felt like...'

'And what does it feel like?' she asked her volatile husband.

'Like living in a storm where everything's magnified and little things assume too much importance,' he groaned. 'When we were on the island it wasn't that I resented the time you spent with the kids, it was that I wanted more of you myself and it wasn't working out that way. Only when you were gone did I appreciate how confused I was, how everything seemed different with you and I didn't understand why until I had the space to think it through.'

'And decided that it was love? Are you sure?' Letty, ever the doubter, questioned.

Leo laughed with unholy amusement as he gazed down into her anxious face. 'Nobody was more shocked than I was to appreciate that I loved you, but then you're a pretty special woman so it's not really that surprising. You didn't want me for my money, except to help your family. You didn't want me for my body.'

'And where did you get that idea?' Letty asked as she began unbuttoning his shirt with alacrity.

'Yes, but it's not only for sex, is it?' Leo studied her. 'Although, if it is, I'm not strong enough to say no, you can't have me until you return my feelings…but do you think you could…*eventually*?'

Not impervious to the vulnerability in his stunning gaze, Letty pretended to ponder and then said, 'Truth is… I started falling in love with you that first day in your office too. There was just something about you and, apart from the commitment phobia, I liked everything else about you a lot.'

'You…*did*? You didn't show it.'

'Obviously I tried to hide the fact that I found you attractive when you told me you were suggesting a platonic marriage,' Letty pointed out. 'But somehow that inappropriate attraction just kept on getting stronger, which is why I probably succumbed on our wedding night.'

'And then I wrecked it all again within hours.' Leo sighed. 'I'm sorry, sincerely sorry that I kept on flip-flopping all over the place like a stranded fish on the shore. I didn't know what I wanted at that point, apart from you, and my brain was still fighting with this concept of sacred bonds.'

'Are you ever likely to let me forget that phrase?' Letty teased as he shed his jacket and his shirt and dragged her down on the bed with him, solely to hold her close, both arms wrapped tightly and possessively round her while she continued to contemplate her glittering eternity ring with satisfaction.

'Probably not. It doesn't feel sacred to me, but then I'm too earthy for that kind of attitude,' Leo murmured apologetically. 'But when you're not there, everything feels uncomfortable and lonely and depressing. When did you see that photo of Dido and me lunching?'

'The first week we were apart,' she said with regret.

'I knew something was wrong, but I didn't want to broach it on the phone. Didn't it cross your mind that only a man in love phones you at least three times a day?'

'Nope... I've no experience of men in love,' she reminded him. 'Oh, Leo, I've been such an idiot—and so unhappy without you.'

'Well, you're truly stuck with me now,' Leo proclaimed with unashamed approval. 'And, what's more, we're likely to have an enormous family because we are going to want to have children of our own, aren't we?'

'You mean, you're actually comfortable with that idea?' Letty asked in wonderment.

'The more the merrier,' Leo assured her. 'I really love the kids. I know I'm selfish sometimes when it comes to you, but I really like having them in our life.'

'That's good because it's likely to be years before you get a baby from me. I want to finish my training first,' Letty informed him gently.

'Enough talking and enough warnings...' Leo covered her mouth with his in a long drugging kiss before breaking free to add, 'We need some mistletoe downstairs. I want to watch my father trying to manoeuvre your mother under it.'

Letty rolled her eyes. 'It's a friendship, Leo...nothing else.'

'Want to make a bet?' Leo was convinced that, whether either party appreciated it or not, their respective parents were getting attached to each other and it was no surprise to Leo that, having finally been exposed to a normal middle-aged and kind-hearted woman, his father was attracted to her after so many years living with a brittle fashion queen many years his junior, who made constant demands for luxuries the older man could rarely afford to provide.

'No, I don't do bets,' Letty told him circumspectly, circling his beautiful mouth with her own, nipping at his lower lip the way he had taught her because, yes, she was a very fast learner in some departments. 'Allow me, though, to know my own mother better than you do...and she said, "Never ever again, that's me done," after divorcing Robbie.'

'You haven't a romantic bone in your body, Letty,' Leo groaned.

'I'll put up the mistletoe for *our* benefit,' she promised. 'Goodness knows, I've got every other Christmas extra on display.'

'Yes, I liked the giant reindeer and the elves.'

'You mightn't like them when you see what they cost.'

'I don't care. It all looks fantastic, like a real home, and I've never had that before,' he told her huskily as he began to snake down the zip on her dress by tiny increments.

'You're breaking my heart, Leo...and being far too cool and subtle—just rip it off!' Letty told him cheer-

fully. 'I love you enough to forgive you anything...
Well, just about...not other women—'

'I've got you, and I don't need anyone else. I love
you more than I ever thought I could love anyone.'

Letty stretched luxuriantly, every romantic bone in
her body that she denied twanging to that announce-
ment but, true to her determination not to get slushy,
she told him he was wearing too many clothes and it
was remarkable how fast he got out of them.

EPILOGUE

SIX YEARS LATER, Letty walked round her London home arm in arm with her mother to check that everything was in place for the important guest they were expecting. It was Christmas Eve and her grandfather, Isidore Livas, was coming to share the big day with them— and that was a development she could never have foreseen years earlier.

'I think Isidore assumed that the mother of his son's child was another disreputable druggie and downgraded all of us accordingly,' Gillian opined, her thoughts in the same place about the older man's coolness on first meeting Letty. 'Once he met me, once he realised how young I was when I gave birth to you, he changed his tune…and then you had Kristo, and a great-grandchild was the perfect gift as far as he's concerned.'

'Yes, he is amazingly attached to Kristo,' Letty conceded, racing across the hall to prevent her son from trying to climb one of the stuffed elves.

At two years of age, Leo and Letty's first child was a livewire, always into everything. George, elderly now, lay in his basket and feebly wagged his tail as they went past.

'Kristo!' Popi called as she came clattering down

the stairs with Sybella on her heels. 'Give Mummy some peace—'

'Your brother doesn't know the meaning of that word,' Letty remarked, watching Popi—at the age of eleven very much a young lady now—impose order on her son. Sybella still loved to dress up and perform, and Letty couldn't help wondering if she would eventually enter the entertainment world. Cosmo was a wannabe scientist, always doing little experiments and peering through a toy microscope.

Embarrassing as it was for a doctor to admit, however, Kristo had been an unplanned surprise package in their lives. In the midst of changing contraception, Letty had discovered that she was pregnant and had thought that it could not have happened at a worse time because she had been facing her final exams. Now she felt guilty for having thought that because Kristo, so much Leo's son, with his beautiful dark eyes and the Livas blond hair, had brought her and Leo so much joy. He had also brought Isidore hotfoot to London with a train set because apparently her unhappy Aunt Elexis was still having problems conceiving.

'Come on, Kristo,' Theon, a laidback and sturdy little boy, said to his kid brother with pity as the toddler pouted. 'We'll watch cartoons.'

'They grow up so fast. You'll probably be planning another soon, I imagine,' Letty's mother commented fondly.

'Maybe next year,' Letty responded with amusement because she lived a frantically busy life and, even six years after marrying Leo, she was still doing some form of training for her work as a GP, the hours she worked in the surgery being the best fit for their life.

Of course, she couldn't have achieved what she had without supportive staff and she knew she was blessed. Five children were a challenge but she wouldn't have had it any other way because she and Leo revelled in the rough and tumble nature of their big family and the warm love that linked them all. Panos marrying her mother the previous year had only extended the family circle. It had taken much longer for the older couple to get together than her husband had believed it would, but Panos's divorce from Katrina had been dragged out and bitterly contested. Still, Leo had spotted the first signs of mutual interest between Panos and Gillian far quicker than Letty had, but then that was classic Leo.

He was shrewd, quick to size up people, even faster at guessing their next step, which was probably why everything he touched in business seemed to turn to gold. He had even recently got his father involved as a director in a project, pretty much, she surmised, to ensure the older man could have a decent income without feeling it was charity. Her husband's relationship with his father was now close and caring.

'Why did you invite Isidore anyway?' her mother asked.

'I think he's quite lonely. Elexis is a bit of a cold fish and doesn't seem to visit him much.'

They wandered into the games room where her half-brothers, Tim and Kyle, were playing video games. Tim was at university now, Kyle studying for GCSEs, both of them well-adjusted and hardworking. Letty often thought back to that very first day she had met Leo and all the very many positives which had flowed from their marriage. It was the icing on the cake that

Leo adored her, supported her and still thought she was somehow special.

For the first year of their marriage she had feared he would suddenly shake off such feelings and appreciate that she was really pretty ordinary but, mercifully, that hadn't happened. Leo's love had all the longevity she had craved, and she was incredibly happy with him.

They spent a lot of the summer on the island of Ios, where the children enjoyed the kind of freedom they couldn't safely have anywhere else. Kristo had been conceived on Ios at the beach cottage where they always went when they wanted to relax alone and he was named for Leo's late grandfather, an honour that went with the proviso that Leo promised never ever to tell their son that marriage and sex were separate entities and mistresses were normal for a Romanos man.

Leo breezed through the door, laden with parcels and bags, and was surrounded by children and even the dog, who made the effort to leave his basket for Leo's benefit. He smiled at Gillian and asked if she and Panos were still joining them for dinner with Isidore that evening. 'We need the support. He's a chilly personality.'

'But we're working on him!' Letty laughed, grabbing Leo's hand as he deposited his bags on a bench seat. 'Come here, you... I've missed you!' she exclaimed, winding her arms round his neck.

'We're not under the mistletoe,' Leo carped.

'As if that would stop you!' Letty told him as Gillian melted discreetly out of the front door, where her husband awaited her.

'They're being *gross*,' Cosmo complained with an eight-year-old's disgust for parents who larked about.

'No, we're taking our kisses *upstairs*,' Leo declared, dragging Letty by the hand towards them.

Popi said something sharp to Cosmo and an argument erupted but Letty still walked away, knowing that she needed stolen moments with Leo and that she had to take them when she could. 'So, what's in all the bags?' she asked curiously.

'Just a few last-minute purchases. I love buying you stuff because you never buy it for yourself.'

'Excuse me?' Letty lifted a brow. 'I bought a very expensive designer dress last week for that dinner you had.'

'Yes…that's what I mean. There has to be an excuse or a special occasion for you to spend, so I do it for you,' Leo intoned with the greatest good cheer as he pulled a diamond pendant out of his pocket and proceeded to fasten it round her neck on the landing.

The sizeable diamond glittered white fire below the lights and she reached up and kissed him, wondering where he thought she was going to wear it because she dressed very sensibly and simply for work and didn't flash her opulent lifestyle.

'You can wear it in bed,' Leo told her as if she had spoken her thoughts out loud. 'That'll make you feel really decadent.'

'No, it's *you* who makes me feel decadent,' Letty confessed, hauling him closer by his tie and reaching up for his mouth, all surging impatience and unhidden hunger for his touch.

And Leo really loved that boldness of hers, the knowledge that she was as hot for him as he was for her and that these days she did make him a priority. They were kissing as they stumbled into their bedroom, madly, passionately kissing and heading in the general direction of the bed.

'Golly…when's Isidore arriving?' she struggled to recall. 'We can't be in bed when—'

'Yes, we can be. I'll have the door shut in his face if he interrupts us,' Leo asserted, gorgeous dark golden eyes welded to her flushed oval face.

'That wouldn't be very hospitable.'

'If he comes between me and my wife, he's unwelcome,' Leo growled, spreading her back on the bed like a feast to be savoured. 'Because I love my wife.'

'And you're insanely oversexed!'

Leo ran a lazy hand through her silky hair where it flowed across the pillows. 'I haven't heard you complaining,' he commented with a blazing smile.

'And I'm not,' Letty confided, a fingertip tracing the line of his sensual mouth, loving confidence in her eyes. 'You make me so happy, Leo. I love you so much.'

* * * * *

COMING SOON!

We really hope you enjoyed reading this book. If you're looking for more romance, be sure to head to the shops when new books are available on

Thursday 12th December

To see which titles are coming soon, please visit **millsandboon.co.uk/nextmonth**

MILLS & BOON

Coming next month

BILLIONAIRE'S WIFE ON PAPER
Melanie Milburne

'But you don't want to get married.' It was a statement, not a question.

A shadow passed through his gaze like a background figure moving across a stage. He turned back to face the view from the windows; there might as well have been a 'Keep Away' sign printed on his back. It seemed a decade before he spoke. 'No.' His tone had a note of finality that made something in Layla's chest tighten.

The thought of him marrying someone one day had always niggled at her like mild toothache. She could ignore it mostly but now and again a sharp jab would catch her off guard. But how could he ever find someone as perfect for him as Susannah? No wonder he was a little reluctant to date seriously these days. If only Layla could find someone to love her with such lasting loyalty.

'What about a marriage of convenience? You could find someone who would agree to marry you just long enough to fulfil the terms of the will.'

One of his dark eyebrows rose in a cynical arc above his left eye. 'Are you volunteering for the role as my paper bride?'

Eek! Why had she even mentioned such a thing? Maybe it was time to stop reading paperback romances and start reading thriller or horror novels instead. Layla could feel a hot flush of colour flooding her cheeks and bent down to straighten the items in her basket to disguise it. 'No. Of course not.' Her voice was part laugh, part gasp and came out shamefully high and tight. Her? His bride of convenience? Ha-di-ha-ha-ha. She wouldn't be a convenient bride for anyone, much less Logan McLaughlin.

A strange silence crept from the far corners of the room, stealing oxygen particles, stilling dust motes, stirring possibilities…

Logan walked back to where she was hovering over her cleaning basket, his footsteps steady and sure. Step. Step. Step.

Step. Layla slowly raised her gaze to his inscrutable one, her heart doing a crazy tap dance in her chest. She drank in the landscape of his face—the ink-black prominent eyebrows over impossibly blue eyes, the patrician nose, the sensually sculpted mouth, the steely determined jaw. The lines of grief etched into his skin that made him seem older than he was. At thirty-three, he was in the prime of his life. Wealthy, talented, a world-renowned landscape architect—you could not find a more eligible bachelor...or one so determined to avoid commitment.

'Think about it, Layla.'

His tone was deep with a side note of roughness that made a faint shiver course through her body. A shiver of awareness. A shiver of longing that could no longer be restrained in its secret home.

Layla picked up her basket from the floor and held it in front of her body like a shield. Was he teasing her? Making fun of her? He must surely know she wasn't marriage material—certainly not for someone like him. She was about as far away from Susannah as you could get. 'Don't be ridiculous.'

His hand came down to touch her on the forearm, and even through two layers of clothing her skin tingled. She looked down at his long strong fingers and disguised a swallow. She could count on one hand the number of times he had touched her over the years and still have fingers left over. His touch was unfamiliar and strange, alien almost, and yet her body reacted like a crocus bulb to spring sunshine.

'I'm serious,' he said, looking at her with watchful intensity. 'I need a temporary wife to save Bellbrae from being sold or destroyed and who better than someone who loves this place as much as I do?'

Continue reading
BILLIONAIRE'S WIFE ON PAPER
Melanie Milburne

Available next month
www.millsandboon.co.uk